Children of the Kalevala

Contemporary American Finns Relive the Timeless Tales of the Kalevala

Lauri Anderson

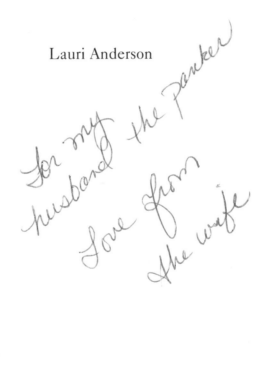

For my husband the Painter
Love from the wife

NORTH STAR PRESS OF ST. CLOUD, INC.

This is a work of fiction. All of the characters, with the exception of Carl Pellonpaa, who really is a host for a TV show, are fictional, and any resemblance to real characters is purely coincidental. Mr. Pellonpaa has done a great deal to support Finnish culture in America. The story in which he appears is meant to satirize fictional iron workers and not meant to disparage Mr. Pellonpaa's character in any way.

Library of Congress Cataloging-in-Publication Data

Anderson, Lauri.
    Children of the Kalevala : contemporary American Finns relive the timeless tales of Kalevala / Lauri Anderson.
      128 p. 23 cm.
      Contents: Uuno Pesonen — Inkeri and Jakko — Eino Pensala — Letter from the Land of Wolves — The Negaunee Order of Suomi Kutsuu Watchers — Erkki and Ahti Lemminkäinen — The Pictures of Ahti — Sarah the Missionary.
      ISBN: 0-87839-119-3 (alk. paper)
      1. Upper Peninsula (Mich.)—Social life and customs—Fiction. 2. Finnish American—Michigan—Upper Peninsula—Fiction. I. Title.
PS3551.N37444C48 1997
813'.54--dc21   97-16932
                                                  CIP

Cover photo: Paul Dwyer

ISBN: 0-87839-119-3

Printed in the United States of America by Versa Press, Inc. of East Peoria, Illinois.

Published by:
      North Star Press of St. Cloud, Inc.
      P.O. Box 451
      St. Cloud, Minnesota 56302

Foreword

I write this foreword for the edification of readers from distant places, such as New York City, Wyoming, or Rio de Janeiro. People in Michigan's Upper Peninsula are called Yoopers. Yoopers live above the Mackinac Bridge, which connects Michigan's two peninsulas. Trolls live below the bridge. All people on Earth who are not Yoopers are Trollish to some extent, but those who live across the border in Wisconsin are called Cheeseheads.

The majority of Yoopers are Finns. Yooper Finns come in great variety, but the stereotype of the male is as follows:

A Yooper drives a very old and very rusty pickup. It's decorated all over with a variety of bumper stickers, which act to hold the pickup together. The stickers support the Detroit Tigers, the Detroit Red Wings, the Green Bay Packers, the Detroit Pistons, the National Rifle Association, the ski jumping at Suicide Hill, and the Mystery Spot outside St. Ignace. The name of the pickup is loudly proclaimed on a plastic bug guard in front of the hood.

Other named family members are the gun in the back window rack, the fishing pole behind the cab seat, the dog, the cat, and the kids. The wife, though, is just called "the wife."

The gun, fishing rod, and dog ride in the cab, and occasionally a sick kid will ride there, too. Normally, though, the wife, kids, and cat ride in the truck bed.

A Yooper's absolute favorite activity is drinking Old Milwaukee at a local bar. A Yooper lives from one beer to the next. For exercise, Eino Yooper frequently challenges Waino Yooper to a drinking contest. Many fights have broken out over who won since neither Eino nor Waino can remember.

When he's sober, a Yooper can go days without speaking, but when he's drunk, he loves to bullshit. He'll talk to anyone and everyone as long as they'll listen. One of his favorite topics is his relations. A Yooper is related to everyone within a hundred miles, or he claims to be. Even if he isn't, he still knows all about the person's sex life, love affairs, jail time, luck at hunting and fishing, and favorite haunts. Eino and Waino might argue for hours over whether or not Eino's mother's uncle is actually Waino's uncle's sister-in-law's cousin.

A Yooper has a nickname that he has earned or inherited. Years can pass while a Yooper answers only to Doink, Poo-Poo, Chummy, Cheese, Dinky, Bricky, Sudsy, Stumbo, Pepper, Dubba, Stubby, Flubba, Dirt Ball, Spitter, Jimmers, Muskrat, or Woodtick.

A Yooper has two jobs. At one he works forty or more hours a week for pay. At the other, for no pay, he fells trees, limbs them, drags the logs to the roadside, cuts them into stove lengths with a chainsaw, throws the stovelengths into his pickup, drives the load home, throws the wood into his yard, splits it with an ax, wedge, or splitter, stacks it, and throughout the cold season periodically hauls it to the house and burns it. The ashes are saved, to be spread on ice for traction.

A Yooper's favorite indoor sport is TV Red Wings hockey. His favorite outdoor sport is deer hunting. Deer hunting consists of drinking a lot of beer with the other guys in deer camp. They also consume a lot of beans and hotdogs. Flatulence abounds.

A Yooper speaks Yoopanese. In Yoopanese, *Matthew went to the store to get three loaves of bread* becomes *Matti went ta da Quality ta get tree loaves a brret.*

A Yooper wears "chooks," "choppers," and "swampers." He "panks" snow.

A Yooper is defined, at least in part, by his relationship to the *Kalevala*, the national epic of Finland. The *Kalevala* is full of heroic backwoods figures who perform great deeds in the pagan world. If a Yooper's life has taken on mythic proportions within the closed world above the bridge, he dies a happy man.

Uuno Pesonen

❦ ❧

Runo XLVI—Battling the Bear

UNO PESONEN WAS BORN on what his parents called "the family farm" in Misery Bay in Michigan's Upper Peninsula in 1943. The word *farm* was a misnomer since the forest came practically up to the log home, its adjoining shed, and the runt of a barn. Without fields, the place could not support animals or a crop, but it was the only farm Uuno Senior could afford on his miner's wages. For several years when Uuno was very young, the family kept a couple of pigs, some bantam hens, and a pair of rabbits. It was a hard-scrabble existence for all of them. Eventually, the Pesonens ate the pigs, the hens froze to death in a winter blizzard, and the rabbits poked a hole in the wiring of the hutch and disappeared into the woods.

Uuno spent nearly all of his childhood on this isolated farm containing three people and a mongrel dog named Musti. The farm sat on a dirt road that paralleled Lake Superior. After several miles, the dirt road led to a potholed and rippled semi-paved road that led to a cluster of buildings called Toivola. Toivola wasn't much—a bar, a gas station, a pasty shop—but at least it was alive. It wasn't one of those broken-down towns like nearby Redridge, which nobody used anymore. From Toivola, it was possible to get to the rest of the world, though most people in Misery Bay were quite content right where they were.

Uuno's dad, Uuno Senior, was a drinker. Some neighbors in Misery Bay had never seen Uuno Senior without an Old Milwaukee in his hand and a pint of Kessler's in his pocket. Uuno Senior was proud of his Finnish heritage and proud of his drinking. Often, he couldn't separate these attributes. "Finns are the greatest people in the world," he'd tell whoever would listen, "because we can outdrink, outfight, and outwork anybody else."

Uuno Senior was a jack of many trades. He had been raised on a small dairy farm and knew animal husbandry. He was a fine butcher, a mechanic, a welder, a mason, a chimney sweep, a woodsman. He had learned these masculine arts from his dad, who had learned them in Finland from his. Uuno Senior knew carpentry especially well and gave Uuno access to his tools when Uuno was still a toddler. At a very young age, Uuno knew that a saw should not be used apart from a square. By four, he could recognize the uses of a level, an awl, a chisel, a hammer, an ax, and a variety of saws. His favorite tool was a hammer. He turned many a piece of wood into a porcupine bristling with nails. Uuno Senior advised his boy again and again to concentrate only on the head of the nail while he was striking. Little Uuno tried to do that, but the day he blackened his thumb with a solid whack from the hammer, Uuno was watching a squirrel at play in the yard. When Uuno fled to his dad for sympathy, he got none. "You stupid *poikka*!" Uuno Senior shouted. "When will you learn?"

Then Uuno ran to his mother, Liisa, who had grown up with six brothers and who was used to crying boys and rough men.

Liisa's father had been worse than rough. He, like Uuno Senior, had a bottle of Old Milwaukee perpetually in his hand. When he drank, he often got violent. He threw things—a bottle, his chair, the radio, his supper. Once he threw a pot of hot spaghetti sauce into his wife's lap. Liisa remembered many evenings when she and her brothers had fled to the outhouse to hide from their father's wrath. They would be crammed together in that small space, the little ones crying while the cold blew in through cracks in the walls and around the door.

ᕗ ᕕ

On a late-summer day in 1944, when Uuno was still a tot and his father was in the service in the Pacific, Liisa decided to go raspberrying in a cutting in the forest several miles from their home. She took along a couple of old blankets, a picnic lunch, a thermos of cold coffee for herself, and some milk for Uuno. She also took along several large empty lard tins for the berries. Then she drove to the cutting in the family's pickup. A solitary giant pine stood in the middle of the cutting, and below the tree the earth was coated with a thick layer of needles that had killed off undergrowth. Liisa left Uuno on a blanket under the tree and moved off into a nearby berry patch. Each time Liisa looked back, he was still there, playing contentedly with a small toy truck. Satisfied that her son was safe, Liisa began to pick in earnest.

In the meantime, Uuno spotted a stick under the pine and

crawled after it. Uuno had only recently learned to walk. With the stick grasped firmly in his hand, he tottered precariously to his feet and teetered in the direction of his mother. He soon reached her. She was bent over a berry-laden bush, intent on filling her tin. She sensed that her child was behind her, but she paid him no mind. Little Uuno heard an odd snuffling sound to his left and turned toward it. A foraging she-bear rose suddenly on her hind legs right in front of Uuno, so close that he could reach out with his stick and prod the creature's belly. A moment later, the bear swiveled and soundlessly slipped away, followed closely by a cub that had been hidden among the berry bushes. A moment after that, Uuno began to scream. He kept on screaming even after his mother tried to comfort him against her breast. He wouldn't let her put him down and locked his arms around her neck when she tried. He emitted a high-pitched wail while his body shook from the rush of adrenaline. Liisa knew that something had terrified her child, but she had no idea what. She couldn't gather up the lunches, blankets, and berries with Uuno locked around her neck like a vise. She brought him to the pickup, left him on the front seat and returned to the pine for their stuff.

Alone in the truck, Uuno continued to scream. He stood up, grabbed the steering wheel for support and peered out the windshield in search of his mother. Just then, the she-bear, followed closely by the cub, loped out of a thicket and rushed, snarling, at the truck. Little Uuno saw her coming, saw her rear up and try to climb onto the hood. He tried to scream louder, but his voice broke, and nothing came out of his throat but a low whistle.

The bear circled the truck once, stopped at the open side window, reared up, thrust her gigantic paw and right forearm through the window, and tried to grab little Uuno. The bear's roar shook the truck, and then Liisa was there. Calling on every ounce of strength in her body, she struck the bear in the back of the neck with a large stick that she had picked up as she ran back from the pine. The bear dropped into a crouch, facing Liisa. The fur at the bear's neck seemed to be standing straight up. The creature's jaws were open, and Liisa could see the long yellow teeth. Somewhere in the back of her mind, she could sense a powerful, musky odor, too, but she was already running toward the back of the truck. She circled the truck, terrified of the imminent arrival of the bear at her heals. She reached the passenger-side door, pushed the latch, yanked at it, got it open and thrust herself inside. Then she pulled on the door and felt the thud of the bear against it just as it closed. Frantically, she reached over and rolled up the other window, accidentally knocking little Uuno to the floor in the process.

The bear's snarling face appeared against the glass on the passenger side as Liisa got the truck started, put it into gear, and drove away. When they turned into their yard, Uuno finally began to calm down. Inside the house, at the kitchen table, Liisa hugged her son for a long time. "It was only a bear," she said to him. "It was only a bear, and now it's gone back to the woods. We're safe here."

Uuno knew that he had seen something huge and terrifying, but he didn't think it had been a bear. His mother had to be wrong. Uuno owned several books with pictures of bears in them. His mother had read those books to him many times. She had even pointed at the pictures of the bears and had talked to him about them. Those bears all wore clothes, lived in a little house, and ate hot *puuroa* from bowls. He wanted to explain this to his mother, but he didn't know the words.

"It's okay, darling," Liisa said. "It can't get us here."

ॐ ᵥ

Uuno Senior had joined the Marines in 1944. At home, he had been the youngest man with a family to support, but, in the Marines, he was considered old. Most of the others were seventeen- and eighteen-year olds fresh out of high school. In February 1945, Uuno was in the third wave to land on the black, volcanic soil of Iwo Jima. The Jap gunners had let the first two waves land with only light casualties, but they opened up with their entire arsenal as the third wave came in. Six of the eleven men in Uuno Senior's squad were killed within one minute of their landing. Uuno made it off the beach but found it impossible to dig a foxhole in the sand. The sides kept collapsing. He finally gave up and lay flat in a hole only eighteen inches deep. Bullets and shrapnel whacked into the ground all around him, sending up small showers of granular beads. Uuno Senior lay there until an officer shamed him into advancing, but, when he stood up, the officer was struck in the head by a round and fell dead. A moment later, Uuno Senior was struck in the thigh. The bullet struck the front of his leg and exited the rear without striking bone. Uuno Senior began to crawl back to the beach as a new wave of Marines was being unloaded. He and a half dozen other wounded Marines were evacuated on the returning landing craft.

Later, Uuno Senior was sent to Hawaii for rehabilitation. He left the hospital with a barely discernible limp a few weeks later and was back in Toivola by Memorial Day. He had been gone less than a year. He never told Liisa about Iwo Jima. When she asked about the scar on his leg, he always changed the subject. Sometimes he would stare into space for a long time while he nursed a beer. He called it "watching the bulkhead." Liisa didn't know what that meant. She did know that he had changed—that some part of him was no longer hers. He was rougher now than before the war, and he drank more. Otherwise, he was the same practical and hard-working Finn she had married.

﹖ ﹖

One afternoon when Uuno was six, Uuno Senior sat the boy on a bar stool at the Mosquito Inn and spun him around and around until Uuno lost his balance and fell with a thump to the floor. Uuno Senior picked him up, slapped off the dust, propped him back on the stool, ordered him to shut up his crying and told him the Finnish facts of life.

"If you're gonna grow up to be a Finn, you gotta be tough," said Uuno Senior. "You gotta work in the mine like me or in the woods from Monday to Friday, and then you gotta drink hard from Friday after work until Monday morning. You'll feel rotten all day Monday, but that rotten feeling is how you can tell you're alive." Uuno Senior spit an exclamation point onto the floor.

When Uuno was a few years older, he asked his dad if everybody lived like that—working hard and drinking hard and spitting in the eye of the world.

"Only real men," Uuno Senior replied.

Uuno wanted to know how he could tell a real man from the impostors.

"Real men all have the same appearance," Uuno Senior explained. "They all smell of wood chips and chainsaw oil mixed with tobacco and booze and sometimes coffee. Real men wear flannel shirts with both elbows ripped out. The sleeves are frayed, and the colors are faded. Plus, they drive pickups and cut their hair with garden shears."

"And what do the phonies look like?" asked Uuno.

"They wear suits!" Uuno Senior replied. "If you ever see a Finn in a suit, watch out. He's probably going to try to sell you something you don't want—life insurance, for instance, or a sermon."

"What about the other kinds of people—Italians, Croatians, Swedes—is it okay if they wear suits?" asked Uuno.

"I'm no expert on them others," said Uuno Senior. "I'm only an expert on Finns."

ᢙ ⤙

Uuno's fondest childhood memories were of fishing with his dad. When Uuno was in the fifth grade, Uuno Senior bought a second-hand canoe from a drinking crony. The canoe was a thing of beauty—a lacquered wooden frame covered with bright green canvas and sealed with a fiberglass coat. Uuno Senior and Uuno dragged it through the woods in back of the family farm to a thicket near a small trout pond on Charlie Bekkala's property. Charlie had posted the pond for years. NO FISHING and NO HUNTING signs speckled the forest around the pond, and the signs were an affront to Uuno Senior. "Charlie doesn't even fish," Uuno Senior reasoned. "Therefore, he has no right to post anything."

Uuno Senior was right. Charlie Bekkala had not fished for decades. Charlie didn't like the sport and didn't like fish. But, as he often said, there was no way he was going to have some neighbor snooping around on his property. "I'd rather have those fish die of old age," he told anyone foolish enough to ask if he had changed his mind about the no fishing.

"Those trout are God's creation, and God created everything for men—for *all* men, not just for Charlie Bekkala! It says so in *Genesis*. I have just as much right to those trout as Charlie does. Hell, I have more of a right. I'm a one-hundred-percent Finn, and Charlie's mother was a Polack!" Uuno Senior said.

After the canoe was hidden in the thicket a few yards back from the pond's shoreline, Uuno Senior went to visit Charlie, ostensibly to dicker over the price of a plow Charlie was selling, but in actuality to check out the view of the pond from Charlie's house. The pond, surrounded by a mixture of hardwoods and spruce, lay in a depression at the far end of a long down-sloping field. While Uuno

Senior and Charlie stood in Charlie's front yard discussing plow prices, Uuno Senior noticed that about a third of the trout pond's surface was hidden behind a small knoll at the far end of the field.

After that, Uuno Senior fished evenings and occasional weekends on the hidden part of the pond. He was always careful not to stray into open water. He often took his son. Both fished with worms, and Uuno soon noticed that they rarely caught anything when the fish were rising. Uuno asked his dad about that.

"The trout are feeding off flies. They don't want worms at such times." Uuno Senior explained.

Uuno had read fishing magazines left about the house by his dad. He knew of artificial flies—wet and dry. "Why don't we use flies?" he asked his dad.

"Real men aren't afraid of getting their hands dirty or of grabbing something squirmy like a worm. Real men fish with live bait," said Uuno Senior.

"But with flies we could catch more fish," reasoned Uuno.

"You listen to me, son," replied Uuno Senior. "We're not using artificial flies to catch fish. If you want to net one of these damned mosquitoes that keep swirling around my face and tie him by the ass to your hook, that's okay, but don't even think about becoming one of those pansy fishermen with bits of feathers and thread stuck on their lines. Thread is for women—so they can secure a loose button or weave a goddamn doily! You know those TV fishermen I sometimes watch—the guys with the L.L. Bean coats and the boats that cost fifty times the price of my canoe? Those guys fish with flies, wearing clean and crisp flannel shirts that haven't even lost their creases. Those guys catch beautiful bass and trout, show them off to the camera, and then throw the damn things back in the water. It apparently never enters the heads of such people that fish are good to eat. Those guys are crazy. That's what fly fishing does to a perfectly normal guy. It makes him nuts!"

For his birthday in July, Uuno asked for a fly rod and a fly-tying kit. His father was furious. "You're not going to turn into a gentleman fisherman and throw the fish back, are you?" Uuno Senior asked.

Uuno explained that his goal was to catch as many fish as possible so he could coat them with cornmeal and fry them for breakfast. Uuno Senior snuffled and spit and a week later bought his son a Japanese fly rod made of lacquered bamboo. His mother bought him the fly-tying kit.

During the remaining summer, Uuno practiced back casting and forward casting, and that winter he spent hundreds of hours perfecting his fly tying.

The following spring, as soon as the ice had cleared off Charlie Bekkala's pond, Uuno and his dad were out there fishing from the canoe. From the first day, Uuno caught trout after trout with dry flies while Uuno Senior fumed at the other end of the canoe and waited for something to bite his worm. "I'd settle for a damned turtle or an eel," he told his son during one particularly vexing afternoon when the trout were rising in swarms all around them. In frustration, Uuno Senior hurled each recently emptied Old Milwaukee can at the ring left by a rising trout. Then he popped open another beer and sat and waited.

On the cool May evening that Uuno caught three rainbow and twelve brook trout and Uuno Senior never got a nibble, Uuno Senior finally exploded from pent-up frustration. He stood up, reached forward and grabbed the bulging gunnysack hung over the side of the canoe. With a roar, he heaved the sack and its fifteen fish into the pond. The heavy sack threw up a mighty splash and sank immediately. Then Uuno Senior reached over and grabbed the tip of Uuno's fly rod and yanked, pulling his son off his seat and into the middle of the canoe. "I'm throwing this damned thing overboard!" Uuno Senior shouted, and he gave another mighty yank on the rod as Uuno let go. Uuno Senior lost his balance and pitched abruptly over the side of the canoe into the frigid water. A moment later, the canoe flipped over too, and Uuno and Uuno Senior found themselves afloat, each holding onto an end of the canoe. They were wearing swampers, heavy pants, jackets, double layers of flannel shirts, and wool caps. There was no possibility that either could swim to shore. If they let go of the canoe, they'd sink like stones straight to the bottom of the little lake.

Fortunately, Charlie Bekkala appeared at that moment along the shore. Charlie stood on a little hummock where the quackgrass thinned and some stunted spruce and cedar were slowly drowning. "Can you get a rope or something and help us get to shore?" Uuno Senior shouted.

"Hell, I'd rather you drown!" replied Charlie. "How many times have you been fishing my pond?" Charlie had an ax in his hand and began to wave it around as if he were a Finnish version of Lizzie Borden.

"One time too many," said Uuno Senior.

After a lot of thrashing around by both Uuno and his dad, the canoe eventually floated ashore where Charlie waited with his ax. Uuno and Uuno Senior stumbled onto dry land with water pouring from their jackets and pants and with their boots squishing loudly with each step.

"I can't feel a thing in my arms and legs," said Uuno, "but my chest feels like it's burning." He collapsed into the tall grass. He tried to take off his jacket, but his fingers wouldn't work the buttons.

Charlie didn't waste a moment. With the ax, he suddenly began to chop holes in the canoe.

"What are you doing?" shouted Uuno Senior. He wanted to throttle Charlie, but he was too cold to move.

"What's it look like I'm doing?" said Charlie. "I'm getting rid of this damned illegal conveyance that stole my trout. I ought to have you and your kid and your damned canoe jailed." Then Charlie glanced toward Uuno and saw that the boy was vibrating all over from hypothermia. "Instead, I'll take you two up to the house and get you some of my barn togs to wear home. If I ever see either of you on my pond again, I'll shoot you!"

Later, after they had changed into some decent, dry clothes at home, Uuno Senior tried to make light of the episode, but Uuno would have none of it. "You lost us my fishing rod, my fish, and your canoe!" Uuno cried accusingly.

Two days later, Uuno sneaked alone down to Charlie's pond. Where alders grew thickly, he found what was left of the gunny sack full of fish. Somehow, it had floated ashore where a raccoon had ripped it apart to get at the fish. The raccoon had eaten all but the backbones and tails.

Uuno and his dad no longer fished together after that, and the next spring Uuno didn't go fishing at all. He'd lost the desire. He turned to building model airplanes and collecting stamps from distant countries. He especially liked to collect stamps from poor desert places like Chad and Niger. He liked the idea that those places had few trees, no water, and no fish.

ᔜ ᔛ

As Uuno reached his teens, Uuno Senior drank more and more but still put in his forty-hour week in the mine without ever missing a day. On weekends, Uuno Senior would be out until the bars closed. Then he'd stagger into the house, drop heavily onto the couch that sat just inside the door, and there he'd be for hours. He'd nurse a forty-ounce Old Milwaukee and sip at a pint of brandy until dawn approached. Then, in an alcoholic trance, he'd stagger off to bed. Occasionally, he'd fall asleep as he sat on the couch, and once he pitched onto the living room floor and began to bellow. Uuno and his mother raced downstairs, fearful that the house had caught fire.

"Get me off this goddamned floor!" shouted Uuno Senior, but Uuno and his mother couldn't lift him, and Uuno Senior was too drunk to help. Eventually, Uuno Senior managed to get up onto his hands and knees. "You'd like to keep me down here!" Uuno Senior screamed at his wife, and he lunged straight for her, still on his hands and knees.

Uuno thought his father resembled a giant spider dashing to engulf its prey. Uuno's mother leaped onto the couch as her husband approached. Uuno Senior was too drunk to slow his own inertia and drove head-on into the base of the couch, knocking himself unconscious.

During the week, Uuno Senior only drank gallons of coffee—thirty or forty cups a day. After work, he often sat at the kitchen table and expounded on the meaning of life. He would mutter about how tough it was just to be alive and how the only pleasure in life came from fixing a roof, cleaning a septic tank, or throwing freshly cut stovewood from the back of the pickup through the basement window into what used to be a coal bin.

"If you get so much pleasure out of house repairs, why don't you ever do any?" Uuno's mother would say accusingly. Uuno Senior would glance at her in silence and sip at his coffee.

☙   ❧

In Jeffers High School, the girl of Uuno's dreams was a black-haired, blue-eyed, half-Italian and half-Finnish beauty named Sandy. Sandy was a junior—the daughter of a widowed, barrel-chested woodsman. Uuno sat often in the back of study hall staring at the back of Sandy's head and dreaming dreams he imagined no mortal had dreamed before. Sandy soon noticed Uuno's interest and invited him out. "I'll pick you up about seven on Saturday night," Sandy said. Uuno wanted to know where they were going. "Does it matter?" Sandy replied, and Uuno's heart began to thump in his chest like a pair of sneakers in the dryer.

On Saturday, a fine sleet was falling, coating roads with a paper-thin layer of ice. Sandy picked up Uuno in her father's three-week-old Oldsmobile, and they headed cautiously for Houghton. They cruised slowly right on through the town and out past Michigan Tech. At the traffic light, where traffic from Sharon Avenue crossed their lane, Sandy never slowed down. In fact, she sped up. Uuno was so surprised that he couldn't speak, let alone shout, as the Oldsmobile slammed into the left front fender of a crossing city garbage truck.

After the city police arrived to survey the damage and to make their reports, Sandy pleaded with an officer to put her in jail. "I can't go home to face my dad," she cried. "Just lock me up and throw away the key."

The officer was surprised by the look of terror in the girl's eyes, but he had no cause to lock her up. True, the car was totaled, but no one had been seriously hurt, and the garbage truck was virtually unmarked. He tried to explain this to Sandy, but, as he turned away from her, Sandy leaped onto his back and locked her legs around his waist. She clutched his uniform collar with both hands behind his neck and began to scream. The officer was choking and tried to pry the girl's hands loose, but her fingers were like a vise. In desperation, he agreed to wait at the scene while she called her dad. Still, she didn't let go until he also agreed to wait with her until her dad arrived.

After she let him go, Uuno tried to reason with Sandy. "Your dad's insurance will cover the damage," he said, and she became even more hysterical.

"His insurance has already jumped from $600 a year to $1,600 since I began to drive!" she cried.

Later, Uuno learned that Sandy had been in two other accidents in the three months she had had a license. In the first one, she had asked her sister in the passenger seat if anything was coming as she shot through a stop sign. As her sister shouted, "Yes!" they plowed head-on into a logging truck. That accident destroyed Sandy's dad's seven-year-old Buick and Sandy's sister's belief in a benevolent God.

In the second accident, Sandy was driving her dad's pickup when she somehow misunderstood a pattern of traffic that had been part of her vehicle experience all her life. She found herself driving the wrong way in the double lane of one-way traffic coming off the Portage Lake Liftbridge in Houghton. She didn't know what to do, so she just kept going, hoping to make it to the other side of the bridge by forcing all the on-coming traffic into the far right lane. Unfortunately, a Hancock police officer was driving across the bridge just as she approached it. He envisioned a disaster impending and stayed in her lane, approaching her vehicle slowly with his lights flashing. Sandy didn't take the hint and drove right into the squad car, totaling the pickup and the car. It didn't help her cause when she ran from her car to the policeman's and pummeled his chest as he tried to get out. "You bastard!" she shouted into his face. "Why didn't you get out of my lane?"

After the third accident, Sandy's dad's insurance shot up to an astronomical amount. "I don't even earn that much! You have twenty-four hours to give up your driver's license or get out of my house forever!" shouted the distraught woodsman. "You choose!"

Sandy went the next day to the Secretary of State's office in Hancock and handed in her license.

"It's more like a weapon than a license, anyway," she told the clerk.

After that, Sandy realized that what she needed more than anything else in the world was a boyfriend who could drive. Uuno was months away from taking Driver's Education and getting a license. Sandy met him in the hall after study period. That weekend she went to a movie with a boy who was three years older than she and who had his own battered 1948 black Ford.

❧ ❧

The following summer, when Uuno was finally old enough to take Driver's Education, he found that he was terrified behind the wheel. Whenever Mr. Kekkonen, the instructor, asked him to drive, panic seized him. His hands shook, his legs went numb, and his heart pounded so hard that its drum beat threatened to pop his eardrums. Worse than anything else, he couldn't breathe because his chest muscles grew rigid and cramped.

As he sat behind the wheel, the world began to close in, burying him under a mountain of fear. His fingers grew white and rigid where they clutched the wheel. He always knew with absolute certainty that either a garbage truck or a she-bear was about to leap viciously out of his side vision directly into the car's path. Mr. Kekkonen refused to understand. He had taught Driver's Education for twenty-four years and had never had a student like Uuno. "Goddamnit, Uuno, a garbage truck can't leap!" he screamed when Uuno tried to explain.

Uuno especially worried about the she-bear because every nerve in his body told him that she was about to leap on the car's hood, smash in the windshield and grab Uuno by the throat. Because Uuno didn't know whether the attack would come from the left or the right, he drove very fast and randomly whipped the wheel left and right. The student drivers in the back seat hugged the floor and prayed aloud, while Mr. Kekkonen, in the front passenger seat, pressed his palms to the top of the dashboard and screamed for Uuno to stop. The car rocked and jerked down the road like a broken-backed, three-legged deer running for its life.

Soon Uuno realized that he could partially control the panic attacks if he tailgated certain senior citizen drivers—the old guys driving thirty-five miles an hour on the main highway in a big car with a big engine. Uuno saw the big car in front of him as a kind of shield. If Uuno tailgated closely enough, the leaping garbage truck would probably land on the other car and the charging bear would be slowed down and confused.

Uuno noticed that some of the tailgated seniors put on their blinkers miles before they had to turn. Uuno tried to do them one better. he put on a blinker as soon as he slid behind the wheel. Mr. Kekkonen wanted to know why. "It's in case we turn any time within the next ten miles," Uuno explained.

Once Uuno kept his left blinker on for eight miles and then turned right. Mr. Kekkonen wanted to know why. "It's to confuse the bear and the garbage truck," Uuno explained seriously.

At the completion of the course, Mr. Kekkonen resigned and moved to South Dakota, leaving no forwarding address.

One of the other student drivers, Eino Saari, was the quietest kid in Jeffers High School. Occasionally, he spoke to other students in the hall between classes or out on the streets of Painsedale, but, in the formality of the classroom, he hadn't spoken a word since the day in sixth grade when he noticed old Mr. Polkkinen, the science teacher, was not nodding off at his desk as he often did but had actually died.

Eino was not anti-social. He would speak in class if he had something worthwhile to say about a worthwhile topic, but, in the last five years, no worthwhile topics had come his way. After Driver's Education class, however, Eino went out of his way to become friendly with Uuno. He had never met anyone as scared as Uuno and figured such a phobia-haunted guy needed him. Previous to that realization, Eino had never felt needed by anyone except possibly by his blind and now fingerless grandmother who had accidentally stuck her hand in the snowblower the previous winter.

Uuno could understand the source of his fear of city garbage trucks—the accident with Sandy explained that—but why was he equally terrified of she-bears?

"You have the worst damned case of ursaphobia I've ever seen," said Eino, who had come across the word years earlier in the *Encyclopedia of Phobias* and ever since had been looking for an opportunity to use it. "I'm not too concerned, though," added Eino. "What's the chance of your meeting a bear when you never go in the woods?"

Eino was right not to be concerned. Uuno had not been in the woods since he had gotten his driver's license, and phantom bears had begun to rush his car from the banks of the road, from behind telephone poles, and from the interiors of telephone booths. Twice Uuno had driven right off the road into thickets because he knew with absolute certainty that a she-bear was sitting in the back seat. Once, just after he had gone through the drive-in line at McDonald's and had a Big Mac and fries in a bag between his legs, he had a vision of an angry bear rushing his passing car from the entrance of the *Daily Mining Gazette*. The bear leaped on the car hood, knocked out the windshield with a single swat from a gigantic paw, grabbed the Big Mac from between Uuno's legs, and ate it, bag and all, in one gulp.

After Uuno told Eino about this last vision, Eino finally showed some concern. "You really do have a problem with bears, and it's connected somehow with the fact that you drive. You're going to have to get counseling or give up your driver's license, or take a hot sauna and roll in the snow," said Eino, who figured that a sauna could cure anything.

Uuno didn't think any of that would help.

"How many bears have you met face to face?" Eino asked him.

Uuno said there were none that he knew.

"Then don't worry about it," said Eino.

"But I can't let this fear just go on. It's ruining my life. I've got to face my fear."

"What do you mean by that?" asked Eino.

"I've got to spend some time with a bear," said Uuno.

"What are you going to do? Sit down and play checkers with the damned thing?" asked Eino.

"Well, what should I do?" asked Uuno.

"If you see a bear? Run! Any sane person would," said Eino.

"But then I'd be showing fear," said Uuno.

"You're damned right," said Eino. "Sometimes fear is a good thing."

Uuno wasn't sure he agreed, but he decided to try running the next time a she-bear appeared.

A week later, Uuno was driving alone past Michigan Tech around midnight. Down the street, one of the fraternities was brightly lit, and music thundered so loudly from the building that Uuno could hear the beat a block away. As Uuno approached the fraternity, a she-bear tore out from the front door and ran across the lawn toward the street.

Uuno was sure that the bear was trying to cut him off, so he floored the gas pedal and shot past the fraternity, leaving the bear behind. He approached downtown Houghton at eighty miles per hour. At the first blinking light, he pumped his brakes frantically and then swerved wildly to the left, narrowly missing the crossing city truck. Uuno then applied the brakes full force and brought the car to a swerving halt in the middle of the street, the rear of the car in one lane, the front in another.

Later, Uuno explained to Eino that he had been too frightened to run. "I didn't want that bear to catch me in the open," he said. "I had a vision of the bear sticking my head in her mouth, lifting me off the ground, and then swatting my body back and forth between her paws as if it were a ping-pong ball."

After that, Uuno gave up driving for the duration of high school. He withdrew from after-school activities and spent more and more time alone in his room. Liisa became worried.

"Why don't you go out anymore?" she asked him over dinner.

"Bears," he said.

"You're not going to become a drunk like your father, are you?" she asked him.

"No," he said.

"Good. I worry about that," she said.

"You don't have to," Uuno replied. "I can't drink. I have to remain fully alert at all times so the bears can't catch me."

"Have some more mashed potatoes," said Liisa.

Other students at Jeffers High School considered Uuno simultaneously intelligent and stupid. They told jokes about him. "Uuno's the kind of guy who will try to draw the Russian Revolution in less than a minute if he's given the word *October* in a game of Pictionary," a classmate said. In French class, when the teacher actually did organize such a game and gave Uuno the words *Eiffel Tower*, he tried to draw a street map of Paris with the quadrants for the tower in the center. "Why didn't you just draw a reasonable facsimile of the tower itself?" the teacher asked.

"Mr. Eiffel already did that when he was designing it," replied Uuno.

ờ ◄§

In high school, Uuno often lectured at his father, trying to slow his consumption of Old Milwaukee. "I'm not interested in the normal chickenshit way of drinking," Uuno Senior would reply. "A glass of wine or a beer before dinner—what good is that? What a waste of time!"

Uuno Senior drank to go to work and worked to get money to drink. It was a vicious cycle. Uuno and his mother could only watch and wait and commiserate with each other.

Then one day, Uuno Senior stopped drinking forever. He fell off a barstool in Houghton and passed out on the floor. The other patrons were too drunk to notice when he vomited, choked, stopped breathing, and fried his brain.

When Uuno and his mother brought Uuno Senior home from the hospital, Uuno Senior had become a doddering old man at the age of thirty-eight. Uuno Senior had lost all short memory and only had long memory to 1951, when Uuno Junior was seven. Physically, Uuno Senior appeared to be normal, but he acted like an invalid on powerful drugs. His movements were slow and jerky, like the sloths Uuno had seen in a *National Geographic* film. Mostly

Uuno Senior sat on the couch in the living room and stared into space. Uuno would sometimes watch him, staring into his vacant eyes. "Hell, he always sat vacant-eyed on that damned couch even before he turned into a zombie," Uuno would say to his mother if she were in the room. "Nothing's changed except now he's sober."

Uuno's mother spent hours filling out the proper forms, and then Uuno Senior began to receive disability checks. The family had more money than they'd ever had when Uuno Senior had worked. "Now that he can't drink them up, we can use his checks to get a few nice things around here," said Uuno's mother. Uuno agreed, but the arrival of each check left a bitter taste in his throat.

Uuno Senior no longer recognized Uuno. He would forget his son's name moments after Uuno had introduced himself. But if Uuno showed his father a picture of Uuno as a small child, Uuno Senior's face would erupt with pleasure, and he'd come alive. "This is my son. His name is Uuno," he would say to Uuno, pointing at the picture.

There must be a certain peace, Uuno thought, in living without much of your past, without your current family, with no debts and no claims.

❧ ❧

Uuno knew with certainty that he did not want to end up like his dad before his accident, working hard in a job he hated. After school graduation in 1961, Uuno journeyed downstate to look for a job. Eventually, he took the only job he could find—shoveling meat scraps in a hot dog factory. Uuno used a hydraulic hoist to lift two-thousand-pound tubs of fat and meat onto a platform and then shoveled the stuff into the maw of a gigantic grinder that turned the meat and fat into a gruel with the texture of oatmeal. Uuno hated the rancid smell of the meat and the maggots that showered off each shovelful of meat.

A month later, Uuno returned home and went to work in the woods. Liisa now spent most of her day watching over her time-frozen husband who would live forever in a world governed by Harry Truman. Uuno longed to escape but felt the pull of responsibility to his mother. Uuno Senior occasionally wandered off into the yard or down the road. Wherever he was, he never seemed to be aware of his surroundings. Most of the time, he sat on the couch and chain-smoked Camels. Sometimes he inadvertently dropped the burning butts onto the floor or the couch. Both were covered with small round burn marks. Uuno Senior's eyes were opaque and seemed to look inward at some invisible glint of light in the center of his brain instead of outward at the world everyone else could see.

One evening in August, Eino showed up at the family farm in Toivola. He had decided to seek Mr. Kekkonen out west in the Dakotas and wanted Uuno to go alone. Uuno had set aside a small savings from his job to buy a new record player, but Liisa thought he should spend the money on the trip. "You've never been anywhere," she told him. "All summer, except for going to work, you haven't once been outside because of your fear of bears. You ought to see a bit of the world."

Eino had little money himself and needed Uuno's small savings just to pay for gas. Uuno wanted to know where they would look for the missing Driver's Education teacher. Eino had no idea. He figured they could just drive around in the Dakotas and try to spot him. "He's just an excuse for a trip," Eino explained. "What I'm really going for is the adventure."

Uuno finally agreed to go as long as he could take his father, too. "I want to relieve my mother of the burden," he said. Liisa resisted the idea until Uuno explained that they would be gone only for about a week. "As soon as we've spent half our money, we'll turn around and come back," he promised.

The next morning, Eino returned in his twenty-five-year-old Chevy pickup. The Chevy had once been green, but the fenders had long since rusted off, leaving brown triangular shards surrounding the tires, like the tines of a saw blade. The rest of the truck had rusted, too, but unevenly. In places, bubbled brown metal met light brown chips that flowed into dull green speckles.

The engine had run through about 200,000 miles, and the belts and hoses had been replaced countless times. The right front brake hose needed immediate replacement once again. It leaked slowly and contained numerous cracks that threatened at any moment to spew fluid over the road. "I've been waiting for a warm day to replace that hose," said Eino. "If we're going out West, we ought to buy a replacement before we leave."

So they drove into Houghton and picked up a new hose at NAPA Auto. Then they returned to the family farm, packed luggage for Uuno Senior and Uuno, and left. They drove west hour after hour with Uuno Senior propped awkwardly between them, his eyes flat and colorless in his uncomprehending face. They crossed the western Upper Peninsula, the top of Wisconsin, and Minnesota that first day. When Eino and Uuno became bored, they pretended it was 1949 instead of 1961 and asked Uuno Senior questions. He would become briefly animated as he described his recent evening drinking at the Mosquito Inn with cronies that, in actuality, he hadn't seen in years. "Who's president?" they'd ask, and Uuno Senior would say Harry Truman was and that it was a real shame that Roosevelt had died before the war ended. If they asked about Iwo Jima, Uuno Senior's face would go blank and hard, and he would return to staring silently out the windshield at the on-coming traffic.

They pulled off the highway into a rest stop late that evening and let Uuno Senior sleep alone in the cab while Eino and Uuno stretched out on an old mattress in the truck bed. The night was warm and peaceful, and they slept deeply. The next morning, they were on the road at dawn and soon crossed into South Dakota. Neither Uuno nor Eino had thought to bring along any tourist maps or road guides, so they had no clear idea where they were going. "Maybe we should look for something cultural, something to broaden us," said Eino.

"I'd rather go mountain climbing," said Uuno.

For the next couple of hundred miles, a stream of bill-boards advertised a place called the Corn Palace in some little town up ahead. The decided to stop there. "Maybe it'll be educational," said Eino.

The Corn Palace was an ordinary-looking building made out of corn. The owners sold T-shirts with I STOPPED AT THE CORN PALACE on the front and the name of the town on the back. The next couple of hundred miles advertised Wall Drug in some other little town up ahead. Uuno decided they should make that their second stop. Wall Drug turned out to be an ordinary drugstore that sold T-shirts with I STOPPED AT WALL DRUG on the front and the name of the town on the back. For a few seconds, Eino thought about buying one of the T-shirts, but Uuno talked him out of it. "You want everyone to know you're dumb enough to stop in a place like this?" he asked.

Eino's stomach hurt as soon as they walked into the drugstore, so he bought some Pepto Bismol. Uuno Senior hadn't spoken since they had left the Corn Palace, but he said, "Jesus Christ!" as they left Wall Drug.

Outside, Eino noticed that the temperature gauge outside the only bank in the town read one hundred and two. "It's warm enough," said Eino.

Uuno was perplexed. "Warm enough for what?" he asked.

Eino gave Uuno one of those looks that said Uuno was being very stupid or forgetful. Then Uuno remembered what Eino had said before they left Michigan. "It's warm enough to fix the brake hose," repeated Uuno.

Eino drove to the edge of town where he pulled off into the parking lot of an abandoned train station. For the next hour, Uuno and Uuno Senior hovered in the narrow shade of the crumbling station platform while Eino worked under the front end of the truck. As Uuno sat there contemplating the vast emptiness all around them, he realized that he had had no panic attacks since they drove into the flatness of North Dakota. "The open spaces have made me a free man!" he exclaimed. "There's no place out here for the garbage trucks and the she-bears to hide. I could see them coming from a hundred miles away. My fear is completely gone."

Eino grunted a noncommittal reply and asked Uuno to get off his ass and pass him a wrench.

Uuno now felt as if a great psychological weight had been lifted from him, but Uuno Senior did not share in his son's excitement. He looked ashen, and Uuno noticed with growing concern that Uuno Senior's stomach was gradually inflating. In fact, his whole body seemed to have filled up with gas, as if he were a human balloon attached to some invisible pump. Uuno Senior wanted to smoke. With great difficulty, he managed to get his pack of cigarettes out of his shirt pocket and a cigarette out of the pack but then he found himself too weak to lift the cigarette to his mouth. No matter how much he strained, he could not get the cigarette higher than the point of his chin. Finally, Uuno slid the cigarette out of his father's hand and put it between his lips. Uuno lit the cigarette, and Uuno Senior managed a couple of weak puffs before he began to choke. Then the cigarette fell from his lips onto Uuno Senior's bursting belly. Uuno rescued the errant cigarette and put it back in his father's mouth, but Uuno Senior spat it out into the dirt. "I'm too tired to smoke," he said.

As soon as Eino had replaced the brake hose, they drove to the nearest hospital. In the emergency room, the attending doctor admitted Uuno Senior, and nurses rushed around attaching various monitors to various parts of his distended body. Fortunately, Liisa had given Uuno the family's insurance plan numbers before the trip. Now Uuno dutifully copied down the information for the desk nurse. Then Uuno and Eino waited in the lobby until a new doctor finally appeared several hours later. "Are you related to Uuno Pesonen?" he asked.

"I'm his son," said Uuno.

"Your father's kidneys and liver have stopped working," said the doctor. "His vital organs are shutting down as his body slowly drowns in its own waste. We drained fourteen gallons of fluid from his abdomen, but he'll fill up again. I assume he has a history of alcoholism." The doctor said this coldly, with scorn in his voice.

Uuno winced. For the first time in a long time, he felt pity—deep pity—for his father. What a horrible way to die, Uuno thought.

"We can't keep him here," continued the doctor. "His insurance won't cover him if he's dying. I have release forms for you to sign."

Uuno signed, and then he and Eino struggled fiercely to carry the inert Uuno Senior out to the pickup and into the cab. They managed to get him propped on the seat but couldn't get his feet in. "Let's put him in the back," said Uuno.

"Okay," said Eino, "but the sun's hot as hell, and we don't have anything to keep him out of it back there."

Together they dragged Uuno Senior to the back of the truck. Then, while Eino held him propped against the lowered tailgate, Uuno climbed into the bed and pulled the dying man backwards into the bed. Then he and Uuno together struggled to get Uuno Senior onto the old mattress. A cap partially shielded Uuno Senior's face from the fierce heat of the sun. "I guess he's about as comfortable as we can make him," said Uuno.

Eino climbed into the cab and started the pickup. Uuno checked the mattress for any errant springs that might be sticking into his father. He also placed a rolled-up shirt under his head as a pillow. Then he, too, climbed into the cab. "It's like trying to move Frankenstein's monster," said Eino as he swung the pickup onto the highway. "How long do you think it'll take him to die?"

"I don't know," said Uuno, who understood why Eino had asked the question but resented the cold way Eino had said it. "It could be ten minutes or ten years. Ask him. He probably has a better idea than we do."

"Hell, he doesn't even know where he is," said Eino. "Maybe not even who he is. His brain is full of ammonia. The thinking part of him, like everything else attached to him, is drowning in waste, in a kind of Clorox."

"It must be horrible not to be able to piss it out," said Uuno. He twisted his head and watched his father through the rear window. "His belly is bulging again," he said. "More than before. He must have twenty gallons of toxic liquid in there. What are we going to do with him?"

Eino said he didn't know. "Let's just drive around and think," he said. "Maybe we should go and get some food. I'm hungry."

"But what'll we do with him?" asked Uuno, who still couldn't believe that his father's life had led to this.

"Maybe he'll eat, too," said Eino. "Even a dying man's got to eat, doesn't he? I'm really hungry. It's way past lunch time."

They found the town's McDonald's, drove through, and ordered burgers, fries, and a couple of Cokes. "If he eats his, that's fine," said Eino. "If he doesn't, at least it was cheap."

As they drove away from McDonald's, Uuno Senior suddenly messed himself. Diarrhea blew all over the back of his pants and shirt, quickly soaked through into the mattress, and soon dripped off the mattress onto the truck bed. Even from inside the cab, Uuno and Eino could smell it. Eino pulled over to the side of the street, and they got out of the cab. They walked to the bedrail and saw what had happened. Uuno Senior's backside continued to emit evil bubbling sounds, and Uuno noticed that his father was silently crying. After that, Eino drove them very fast to the hospital.

At the hospital, the same doctor who had released Uuno Senior earlier now re-admitted him. Uuno wanted to know why. "He's now suffering from a life-threatening case of diarrhea," said the doctor. "His insurance will cover that because it's different from just dying."

Uuno Senior's organs were about to shut down. Several nurses cut off his clothes and hosed him down. Uuno Senior gasped for breath as his lungs filled with liquid. A nurse gave him tranquilizers to calm him down, and then he died.

Uuno and Eino went out to the pickup and removed the befouled mattress from the bed. They stuffed it into a dumpster and returned to the emergency room to borrow a blanket. Then they had to argue for a long time with hospital officials before they were finally allowed to take Uuno Senior's body outside and lay it in the truck's bed.

They drove to a hardware store and bought a large trash receptacle, large trash bags, rolls of tape, rope, and markers. They returned to the empty parking lot of the abandoned train station and sealed Uuno Senior inside several layers of plastic bags. They sealed the bags with tape and then squeezed the body into the plastic trash receptacle. Because of the heat, the body was still limber. They taped the plastic container and then wrapped it tightly with the rope and tied it in thick knots. "It's too heavy for the post office," said Eino. "Maybe we should just drive back with the body."

"I'm not going back," said Uuno. "I like it here. My phobias are gone. Maybe I can find a job driving a garbage truck or something. I hear garbage men get good money, and the hours are good. They're all done by early afternoon. Plus, I'd be facing my fear."

They drove to a liquor store that served as the Greyhound bus terminal. They filled out the freight forms, paid the charges, and watched as Uuno Senior's body was shoved into the back of the luggage hold of an eastbound bus. "Maybe we should have insured him," said Eino.

"Insurance companies are bloodsuckers," said Uuno.

As soon as the bus left, they split the little money they had left. Eino had decided to continue west. "Maybe I'll head for Butte," he said. "I hear there are Finns there."

After Eino and the old pickup disappeared into the distance, Uuno found a phone booth and called home. Liisa cried a little when he told her about the death of her husband. He told her to expect his body at the Greyhound station in Houghton in a day or two. "Where do you suppose he is now?" Liisa asked.

"Probably a few miles east of here," said Uuno.

"I meant . . . is he in heaven or hell?" said Liisa.

☙ ❧

Eventually, Uuno Senior's body arrived at the Greyhound station in Houghton. The dispatcher called Liisa and apologized for the delay. "Apparently your package went to Tampa by mistake," he told her.

Liisa had the body sent directly to a local funeral home for cremation. Several days later, she received Uuno Senior's ashes inside a brass urn that matched nothing in her home. She put the urn in the trunk of her car and kept it there as a kind of good luck charm for when she had to travel on stormy winter nights.

In February of the following winter, Liisa's Ford slid off the road on her way into town. The front end was buried in the snowbank and the rear sat on ice. After several minutes of soul-searching, Liisa got out of the car, unlocked the trunk, took out the urn, unscrewed the top, and spread the ashes behind the tires. She put the empty urn back in the trunk, slammed it shut, and got back in the car. When she put the car in gear and stepped on the gas, the ashes did their magic. The tires got traction, and soon she was free of the snowbank with the car idling in the middle of the road.

Liisa felt the weight of the cold and silence that surrounded the car, but inside she felt warm and close. "Thank you," she said to her dead husband. Then she drove on.

Inkeri and Jakko

*A Confusion of Directions and Roles:
A Fair Maiden Goes North to Find Adventure
and Love While Warrior Men Go South
For the Same Reason*

NIITO PAKKALA GREW UP on the tip of the Keweenaw Peninsula in Michigan's Upper Peninsula. Niito's dad, a second-generation Finn, was a logger. During the twenties, Niito's dad had built a tiny four-room house about a hundred feet beyond the turnaround that marked the end of Route 41 at the beginning of Lake Superior. The house had no indoor plumbing and no electricity. Niito was one of eight children squeezed into that little house, and it was a hard-scrabble existence right from the beginning. Niito's dad leased woodlots at the tip of the peninsula, but many of the trees were stunted and wind shorn. Two hundred fifty or more inches of lake-effect snow each winter made cutting at that time of year impossible. For much of the year, the family survived on whatever odd jobs the logger could find. During each logging season, the family's fortunes depended entirely on the often inadequate scaling chits from various mill yards.

Like the four brothers and sisters who had preceded him, Niito dropped out of school after the eighth grade. That was in 1939, and Niito immediately went to work in the woods. He, his dad, and two of his brothers dropped the trees with bucksaws and limbed them with axes. They used horses to drag the logs to the roadside, where they sawed them into hundred-inch lengths and loaded them by hand onto the truckbed for the ride to the mill. All day, Niito and the others sawed and chopped, and, at night, they spent hours sharpening saw blades and turning the grindstone to sharpen the axes. Niito was probably the handiest of the sons with an ax, but a log swung on the truckbed and struck him in the back in the spring of 1941, and after that, he couldn't lift. "You're no good to me and your brothers," his dad said. "You're just in the way. Find something else to do."

When his back healed sufficiently, Niito took a welding course at a training center in Hancock. Shortly after completing the course, he met a couple of ex-school friends from Calumet. Just like Niito, the Calumet guys were a bit rough around the edges. They ended most sentences with *ey* as in *hey* and wore thread-bare

27

work pants and shapeless caps. They had just returned from work in the oil fields of Wyoming. The war had begun, and they were going into the Army. "You should go out to Wyoming," they said. "They really need welders out there."

One of Niito's brothers was going into the service, too. He told Niito that he could have his car. Niito said good-bye to his family and headed west by driving straight south on Route 41. Route 41 was the only road that existed at the end of the Keweenaw. It was the only road that people like Niito had ever driven. Since Niito had never been on any other road in his life, there was no way, when he was on his own for the first time, alone and full of trepidation, that he was going to venture off it. He had no road map. Since he had never previously been anywhere, it had never occurred to him that he would need one. He assumed that whatever was out there in the rest of the world could be reached via Route 41.

By the time Niito reached Tennessee, he had been driving pretty much nonstop for several days. He was exhausted, disoriented and embittered. He suspected that he would never find Wyoming. "Maybe it doesn't exist," he said aloud to himself. "Maybe it's only in cowboy movies." At a gas station, Niito asked the attendant how far it was to Wyoming, and the guy acted like Niito was crazy, so he didn't ask again.

Several hours later, in central Tennessee, Niito fell asleep at the wheel, crossed the embankment and slammed into a tree. The collision woke him up. After a moment or two of not understanding where he was or why a tree was encased in the middle of his car's hood, Niito fished the keys out of the ignition and tried the doors. Both were sprung, and neither would open more than six inches. Niito crawled through the broken driver-side window and dropped to the ground. He had bruised a couple of ribs and had several small cuts on his face and hands, probably caused by flying glass. Otherwise, he was okay. He opened the trunk and removed his suitcase. He was about to return the keys to the ignition when he thought better of it. "If I leave 'em in there, someone will steal the car," he said to himself. So he walked away with the keys in his pocket. Only much later did he realize how lucky he was to be alive and virtually unhurt.

Having no destination, Niito hitched rides and went wherever the drivers were going. Eventually, he was dropped off at a little place called Buffalo Valley. "The name of this place is as close as I'll ever get to Wyoming and the Great American West," he told the driver who had driven him that far. He thanked the man and set out to find a place to sleep.

For a few weeks, Niito held a series of odd jobs in gas stations, a junkyard, and an animal shelter, but soon all the young men had been drafted into the Armed Services, and jobs were available for the asking. Niito's weak back made him 4F, and he soon landed a permanent job as a forklift driver in a lumber yard. In a bar one night, he met a lonely local girl named Melody, who was proud to be a hillbilly. "Corn pone, black-eyed peas, and fatback—that's my kind of living," she told him.

Niito married her and settled down. They soon had a daughter. Niito insisted that his Finnish roots be kept alive through the girl. He named her Inkeri.

Niito wanted his wife to learn to cook some Finnish dishes, but she refused. "I was raised on Southern cooking," she said, "and I'll die a Southern cook." Niito was forced to improvise. When he wanted pickled fish, he bought a jar of Milwaukee's Kosher Dill Pickles and poured the juice over the fried catfish his wife served him weekly. He missed *nisu* and other sweet breads his mother had once made for him. He bought cardamom and added it to his wife's cornbread, but it wasn't the same. Plus, when he tried to feed the stuff to little Inkeri, she spat it out.

Niito wanted his daughter to grow into a one-hundred-percent Finnish woman, but he was thwarted right from the beginning. His wife took the girl to the same Baptist church that she had attended all her life. His wife fed the girl a steady diet of Southern cooking—fried chicken, fried catfish, black-eyed peas, collards, fatback, and cornbread. She also instilled in the girl a love of the Tennessee hills and a Southern drawl.

When she grew old enough, Inkeri went to the public library and checked through the phone books of Nashville, Knoxville, and Memphis, but she could find no one else with her name. "I must be the *only* Inkeri in Tennessee," she told her mother. "Maybe the only one in the whole world!" Her mother told her that was nonsense, that lots of girls in some place called Upper Michigan had that name. "They must hate the name, too!" replied Inkeri.

For her fifteenth birthday gift to herself, Inkeri decided to change her name to one she liked—one that sounded Hollywoodish. After long self-debate, she chose "Dakota," but, out of deference to her father, she spelled it with two *a*'s and accented it on the first syllable. "I'm *Daa*kota Pakkala," she would tell strangers in her lilting drawl.

Daakota did what hillbilly girls were supposed to do and got married at sixteen. She had always dreamed of being an actress and starring in adventure films as Sheena Queen of the Jungle or as Tarzan's wife. Instead, she married the popcorn vendor from the theater where she hung out on Friday nights. At first, she liked playing housewife, but soon her eighteen-year-old husband was drafted into the Army and Daakota had no idea when or if he would ever return. She hated being alone at night in their little apartment. The whole idea of being married to a distant soldier bored her. She filed for divorce and moved back in with her parents, but her father continued to call her Inkeri, and this caused problems. "I'm Daakota now, and I'm always going to be Daakota, so get used to it!" she shouted at him, but he paid her no mind.

While Daakota waited for the divorce to become final, she took a girlfriend's advice and read *Gone with the Wind*. "It'll change your life," the girlfriend said, and it did. Daakota began to prowl for men every night while playing the role of Scarlett O'Hara. She couldn't afford the kind of clothes that Scarlett wore, so, instead, Daakota began to wear loose cotton dresses with large flowery patterns mixing pinks, purples, blues, yellows, and reds. She called the men she picked up in bars her "gentlemen callers," and she pretended she had to get back to the plantation after each one-night stand in a hotel with a Bubba or Bobby Lee.

Soon Niito told his daughter to get a job or get out. "I'm not in the used-wife business," he told her. "Why don't you get a job as a housekeeper or as a nanny? Generations of Finnish girls have done that."

"I'm not that common," Daakota replied. She got a job washing dishes in the county home for the senile, the microcephalic, and the harmlessly demented. In her spare time, she began a hobby of collecting Campbell tomato soup can labels, which she put in scrapbooks between ironed sheets of waxed paper. She also preserved Saltine crackers in multilayers of varnish. She glued these in other scrapbooks and labeled each with its date and place of purchase.

On a particularly hot August afternoon at work, Daakota dropped a tray of crockery and broke her big toe. A doctor put the toe in a cast, and Daakota continued to work, hobbling about in an odd, lopsided fashion. Her lopsidedness injured her back. She had to quit work and sued the county for her job-related injury. Within the month, her toe was out of its cast, her walk became normal, and her back no longer hurt, but, by then, lawyers were involved, negotiations were underway, and Daakota ended up with six hundred dollars per month for the rest of her life. The lawyers got even more. With her new-found wealth, Daakota decided to leave home.

"Where will you go?" her mother asked.

"I figure I'll go up north to Dad's part of the country," she replied. "Maybe people up there won't laugh at a Finnish name like Inkeri," she said.

A month later, in the Mosquito Inn bar in Michigan's Copper Country, Daakota met a local Finnish guy named Jakko Jokela. Jakko had grown up on the Houghton Canal road—the eighth son in a family with fourteen children. Jakko hated his name. In school, other kids would say that "Jakko was a yoke," pronouncing the *J* of his name with its Finnish *Y* sound. If Jakko talked too much or too fast, the other kids would say, "Jakko yak yak." Daakota, however, really liked Jakko's name. "It has authenticity," she said. "It really defines who you are. A Tom or a Bill is just a Tom or a Bill, but a Jakko is a Jakko."

Jakko thought that was really profound. He also thought Daakota was an odd name, but he really liked Inkeri. "I have an aunt with that name," he said.

From that moment, Daakota stopped being Daakota and became Inkeri again. "My daddy would be proud of me," she told Jakko.

Jakko was twenty-seven and had never paid income taxes. He had always worked at odd jobs as a "go-fer" for various brothers, several of whom were carpenters while others were masons, roofers, loggers, and welders. Daakota had never heard of a vocation called a go-fer. Jakko explained. "If my brother needs a hammer, I *go for* it. I get stuff for the boss—a tool, a sheet of drywall, some more nails."

Inkeri was delighted to hear that Jakko had a brother who was a welder. "My daddy was a welder, too," she said, sensing that she and Jakko had a lot in common—that they were destined to share lives.

Jakko had never had much money. He lived on Misery Bay in a tent in the summer and bummed couch space in the homes of various brothers and sisters in the cold months. He spent a lot of his time going to church. He had learned years before that almost every night some church somewhere in the Copper Country was having either a supper or a pancake breakfast or a Martha and Mary Society lunch. He had also learned that all the churches served endless quantities of good coffee, especially the Finnish Lutheran ones, and that no church would show him the door if he couldn't pay. "It wouldn't be the Christian thing to do," he told Inkeri, who began to attend those meals regularly with him. She had also begun to share his tent, pushing aside the free tracts he had picked up at church meals. "What do you want with these things?" she asked him, glancing at a stack of two hundred year-old copies of *The Watchtower*.

"They light my kindling," he said. "Plus I stuff them inside my clothes when it's really cold. Those tracts keep me warmer than long underwear would."

Jakko had grown up with an overabundance of religion. His parents had been raised in the Lutheran Church of America—Suomi Synod—but they found that sect much too bland. "Religion is supposed to make a person feel anxious, frustrated, and guilty—especially guilty," said Jakko's dad.

Jakko's mother agreed. "Lutherans are supposed to be ravaged by guilt. Otherwise, they're apt to commit enormous crimes," she said. "The LCA is not succeeding in instilling enough of it. I have room for lots more after every service."

Jakko's parents continued to attend their Lutheran church because the coffee after the service was strong enough to float a bullet, the *nisuleipä* was delicious, and the service was sometimes said in Finnish. They also joined some one-hundred-percent American churches—the Seventh Day Adventists, the Jehovah's Witnesses, and the Worldwide Church of God. The parents liked all three because they instilled massive doses of guilt into their congregations and because all three insisted that the world would soon end.

The parents saw these apocalyptic teachings as a good way to make all fourteen of their children toe the line. "Be responsible now, for the end is near," one would say to Jakko and his siblings, and the other would add, "Yes, and the end will probably be your fault for screwing around."

Jakko's brothers and sisters took these heavy doses of religion to heart and grew up to be God-fearing, guilt-wracked, practical citizens. Jakko, however, saw no purpose in accomplishing anything since the world would soon end. He tried to enjoy the little things in life while he still had the opportunity. He defined the little things as the consumption of thirty or forty cups of coffee a day, the consumption of a six-pack of Old Milwaukee in the evening, and the eating of a pickled ring bologna with Saltine crackers when he could afford it.

Jakko and Inkeri shared tent and couch space for four years. Inkeri always felt squeezed on a couch, but she really enjoyed their tent life. On clear nights, the sunsets were magnificent over Lake Superior, and the nights were alive with stars. On those romantic tent nights, Jakko and Inkeri produced four children—Matti, Markku, Luuki, and Jussi. The last two were twins. During those years, Jakko and Inkeri did little work, paid no taxes, and depended on the good will, handouts, and hand-me-downs of Jakko's many brothers and sisters for food, shelter, and clothing. Jakko's go-fer jobs paid for their evenings in local bars. They liked to play shuffleboard and darts while their kids ran across tables, thumped the jukebox, yowled, and played baseball or soccer with peanuts in the shell.

Inkeri still dreamed sometimes of becoming a movie star. Sometimes in the early morning, she would leave Jakko and the kids asleep and drive somewhere for coffee. Usually, she chose the Kaleva Cafe in Hancock or the Suomi restaurant in Houghton. Occasionally, she sat in the Tapiola Diner. She drank cup after cup of coffee since the price was the same whether she had one cup or twenty. She dreamed of being discovered—right there, on the stool by the counter or in the back booth—by a Hollywood scout who had come to northern Michigan to see the Mystery Spot near St. Ignace or to see Douglass Houghton Falls.

Eventually, Jakko, Inkeri, and their kids were no longer welcome at local bars, at any of Jakko's relatives', or at church meals. "You two are nothing but damned leeches," Jakko's oldest brother told them. "I don't want to see any of you around here again. I hate to do this because I feel sorry for the kids," he added.

Jakko and Inkeri were living in the tent at Misery Bay at the time of their shunning, and Inkeri, in particular, felt the effects. Jakko seemed to be able to live forever on ring bologna, sardines, pickled herring, and crackers, but Inkeri yearned every day for a hot meal. They had almost no money, but cabbage and American processed cheese food were cheap, so she boiled a cabbage, put a ring bologna on top of it in a deep dish, and then drizzled cheese all over the top. She placed it by their fire, and, when it was heated through, they ate it.

Such culinary delights were not enough for Inkeri. Plus the kids were driving her crazy. She was always worried that one of them would get lost in the woods or fall in the lake and drown. One day in July 1966, while Jakko was cadging drinks at a Houghton bar, she hitched a ride with her kids to the Mosquito Inn. While her kids ran around causing chaos, she flirted with a stranger from Chicago who seemed interested in what she had to offer but who said he was waiting for his girlfriend, a local nurse. He said his name was Richard Speck and that he had been dating the nurse for several months. Inkeri judged the guy to be warm and caring. He said he had been working the freighters on Lake Superior but that he had had a fight with another sailor and had been kicked off the boat in Houghton. He said he was planning on returning to Chicago in a day or two, and he wondered if Inkeri would go with him. "The nurse is not interested," he said.

Inkeri said she had no money. The sailor then produced a wad of bills from his pocket and gave Inkeri enough for a bus ticket for herself and her kids. "Plus here's some spending money," he said. Inkeri said she didn't want to take his money as she put it in the pocket of her jeans. "It's not my money anyway," said Speck. "It's the nurse's. She loaned it to me."

An hour later, Inkeri returned with her kids to the tent at Misery Bay. The first thing she did was to take back the name Daakota. Then she took down the tent, rolled it into a tight ball with their clothes inside, tied it, hitched a ride into Houghton for her and her kids, and she and the kids got on the bus for Chicago.

They didn't stop in Chicago. They got on another bus and rode straight through to Tennessee. She and her four kids surprised her parents, arriving at their home just after breakfast. After the usual greetings, Niito became firm. "Inkeri, you can't stay here," he told her. "Four little kids would drive me and your mother crazy."

"I'm Daakota again," replied Daakota. "I won't answer to the name Inkeri ever again!"

"It's a good Finnish name—an old-country name. It links you to the past and to my family," said Niito for perhaps the thousandth time.

"I don't want to be linked to it," said Daakota. "In fact, I'm dropping the added *a* and the first syllable emphasis. From now on, I'm going to be just plain *Dakota*—one hundred percent American! To hell with Finns and Finnishness!"

That afternoon, while the kids stayed with their grandparents, Dakota toured local bars, searching for a one-hundred-percent American man who could support her and her children. The process took longer than she thought it would. She didn't find a good prospect until nearly midnight. The guy's name was Jean LeBlanc. He was originally from a little southern Louisiana town named after a saint. He liked to eat very hot gumbo with crawdads and to dance the reel. He spoke with a funny accent, but his people had been in North America since before 1700. Even better, he owned a Ford Mustang and a house on Maple Street. "I guess you're about as far from being a Finn as it's humanly possible to be," Dakota told him. "Plus, nothing's more American than owning a house on a street with a name like Maple," Dakota added when she went home with Jean to spend the night.

Back in Michigan, Jakko turned thirty-two and had still never paid income taxes. He lived alone and was without prospects. For the remainder of the summer and into the fall of 1966, he worked as a go-fer with the brother who was a mason. Now that he no longer showed up at a sibling's door as one of a party of six, his various brothers and sisters welcomed him once again and let him sleep on the couch.

His life was pretty much as it had always been, but now he felt terribly alone. He didn't miss Inkeri or the kids, but he missed the general idea of having a woman around—especially at night. One evening at the Mosquito Inn, Waino Partanen passed around a magazine with dirty pictures and with ads for mail-order Oriental brides. Jakko wrote down the address of one of the girls—a Filipino woman from Manila—and sent her a letter and a picture. The picture showed him five years younger and made him better looking than he was. The woman wrote back quickly, and they began a correspondence. The woman sent him a picture of herself in a see-through red silk nightgown. Her hair was blown about her face, and her lips were puckered. "You can have me every night if you'll just come over here and marry me," said the caption.

"If you go other there, take an ax," Jakko's brothers advised him. "If things don't work out, you can use it to protect yourself. If someone steals your wallet, you can use it to earn some money."

In the summer of 1967, Jakko flew to Manila. He was met at the airport by his future bride and her many relatives. They all rode in a caravan of taxis to a Catholic church where the Filipino and Jakko were married. Jakko had only been in the Philippines for about thirty minutes, and he already had eighty-five new in-laws, all of whom wanted to come to America.

Jakko and his wife rode in another taxi to the American Embassy to find out what he had to do to take his new bride and her family home to Michigan. "That's easy," said the government official. "All you have to do is prove that you can support her and the others. Show us a copy of your income tax return, and you two can be on your way."

A day later, Jakko left for the United States. He knew he couldn't return to Michigan. He had told too many people about his Filipino bride, and now he felt like a fool returning alone. Plus, there was nothing there for him anyway. He wouldn't miss those lonely nights on various couches or the low wages his brothers paid. In San Francisco, Jakko got off the plane and sat for hours in the airport. The airport was full of constantly changing groups of young men in uniform who were just back from Vietnam. There were also a lot of garishly dressed young men and women in clusters throughout the building. They were not a part of the regular passengers, who came and went rapidly. They seemed to be living there. They had taken over sections of the waiting rooms and hallways. Some were painted like wild Indians on the warpath. Others looked like early settlers. Still others looked like no one Jakko had ever seen in movies, in comic books, or in Upper Peninsula bars. Jakko was drawn to them. They looked like the kind of people who were open to accepting someone like him—someone with a green-and-yellow John Deere baseball cap, a red-and-black-checked flannel shirt, jeans, swampers, and with a double-bladed ax on his shoulder.

A red-headed girl in one of the groups was dressed all in black except for a bright-red scarf that she had tied around her throat. She suddenly stood up and waved at Jakko. "Hey, Paul Bunyan, come over here!" she shouted.

Jakko adjusted his John Deere cap, hefted his ax, and then moved in her direction.

Eino Pensala

⤞ ⤝

*A Contemporary Väinämöinen
Makes Magic with Music*

FIFTY-TWO-YEAR-OLD EINO PENSALA sat one June 1996 morning at the yellow formica table in his kitchen. Eino was sipping at his fourth cup of strong black coffee. The formica table had once been Eino's mother's, and, before that, it had been his grandmother's. The table was still as strong as the day it was borne out of an Ohio factory shortly after World War II, but the plastic on the matching chairs had gone brittle and split. Now the chairs were held together by yards of red duct tape that Eino had wrapped around and around the backs and seats.

The remainder of the kitchen also reflected Eino's grandmother's taste and Eino's own attempts to keep the past forever alive through half-hearted repairs. The kitchen cupboards had been built by Eino's grandfather, following specifications laid down by Grandmother. The dishes in the cupboards were still the same ones Grandmother had purchased decades earlier, probably in the 1930s. Even the cracked and clearly glued sugar bowl on the table was originally hers.

In the living room, Grandmother's couch, the cushions now threadbare and faded, still faced her piano. The piano had stood mute since Aili, Eino's mother, had last played it in the 1960s. Now the piano was hopelessly out of tune. On top of the piano were dozens of shadowy black-and-white pictures of people from another era—most of them portraits of relatives or friends of Eino's grandparents. Some of the stiff figures Eino did not recognize, and the others he barely remembered.

On this particular morning at his home in the Traprock Valley in Michigan's Upper Peninsula, Eino was surprised because his thoughts had fluttered back to before his birth—to his mother's teen years. Almost against his will, his thoughts focused on his mother at fifteen in 1942. Aili had told Eino about her youthful follies many times when she had been alive, but Eino had not thought about what she had said for many years. Now he couldn't get her stories out of his head, and he wondered what the stories had to do with this present predicament, with the emptiness that seemed to fill his future.

Eino's mother, Aili, had fallen in love with a neighbor boy in high school, and the engaged couple had been inseparable until the war claimed him. He had been killed on Guadalcanal. In the weeks following his death, Aili had sought to relieve her overwhelming grief by sleeping with each local boy who was called into the Armed Forces. When she later learned that some of those boys had been killed in battle, she felt an immense sorrow and thanked God that she had been able to give each a moment of pleasure before he died. "I saw the face of God in each man," she later told Eino when she talked about her promiscuity.

During the war, Eino had been born. "I don't know who your father was. He could have been any of those doomed young men," she told him. "After your birth, I knew it was all a part of God's plan. My fiancé died so that I would help to save the others. The others died so that you would be born. And you were born from a doomed father so that you would be all mine."

And Eino had always been hers, he now realized. After his birth, his mother had wrapped herself in the certainties of the conservative Wisconsin Synod of the Lutheran Church. The pastor was understanding. He treated Aili the same as he treated the other young women of the congregation who were now widows with babies to feed. "The world makes no sense unless God is the center of everything," the pastor told Aili during counseling sessions shortly after illegitimate baby Eino was born. "A perfect God created this world, and, therefore, this is the best of all possible worlds. Everything happens because it is God's will."

When Aili questioned this reasoning, the pastor told her that she had to accept her fiancé's death as part of God's plan. "God wanted your fiancé to die. Otherwise, it wouldn't have happened," he argued. "It was part of God's perfect plan. God also wanted your child to exist. That's why you became pregnant. Without God as its constant driving force, the world is mere chaos—without meaning or purpose. You must accept God into your life."

Aili was only seventeen when Eino was born in 1944, and she was still living with her parents. She still went to sleep every night in the same bedroom that she had called her own since birth. To support her son, Aili dropped out of school and took a job as a clerk in a pharmacy shop in Coppertown. The shop included an ice cream counter and soda fountain. In the afternoons, high school students came in to buy flavored Cokes, sundaes, and cones. Aili admired their exuberance and the light way they teased each other. For the first few years in the shop, she knew most of the young customers, but later she became a stranger even to herself.

Aili's parents had built their own log farmhouse on a dirt road in the Traprock Valley in the 1930s. The main house was spacious, and Aili never felt crowded by the presence of her parents; they, in turn, rarely seemed to mind that she never left home. She had no expenses to speak of, so she saved nearly all of her salary from her clerkship. She banked the money so that Eino would not have to worry about finances when he grew up.

Except through the church, Aili had little social life. She attended services every week, did a lot of volunteer work through the church, and became the loudest voice in the choir. She instilled her pastor's certainty about life into little Eino. She read her son all of *Uncle Arthur's Bedtime Bible Stories* and insisted that the child accept the truth of them literally. "If Moses had a conversation with a burning bush, then he and the bush chatted," she told Eino when he questioned how a bush could talk.

Aili carefully controlled Eino's upbringing. Her parents' farmhouse was isolated, so she didn't have to worry about bad influences from playmates. He had none. She forbade him movies and TV, along with popular music and most comic books. She allowed Eino to read books about his Finnish heritage and about the church. Because she didn't want him to be completely unworldly, she also allowed him to read Donald Duck comics.

Eino fell in love with the *Kalevala* and read his favorite parts again and again. His mother tried to get him to read his Bible, but he preferred Väinämöinen to Moses and secretly admired Louhi, the witch of North Farm.

Eino loved the way that Väinämöinen created magic with his music. He played the kantele with such power that the sun and moon stopped to listen, and when Väinämöinen was challenged, he sang Joukahainen into a swamp. Eino wanted to be able to do that to anyone he didn't like. One Christmas, he asked for a kantele, but his mother had no idea where to find one. She visited the only shop in the area that sold musical instruments, but no one in there had ever heard of a kantele. The clerk recommended bongo drums. Aili bought a pair and placed them under the tree late on Christmas Eve. Eino was up by five-thirty on Christmas morning, immediately found the drums, and began to beat them with all his strength while singing incantations from the *Kalevala*. He continued to beat on the drum until ten, when he went into the kitchen to eat breakfast. While Eino chewed on *nisu*, Aili removed the bongo drums to the barn and chopped them up with an ax. When Eino protested, Aili forced her son to read the collected works of Martin Luther and John Calvin, and he reread his stack of Donald Duck comics.

Eino grew toward manhood with a kind of hard born-again evangelical outlook on life mellowed by Walt Disney. When Eino was in a dark mood, he sometimes quoted Calvin or Luther, but, in rare moments of lucid optimism, he found wisdom in Huey, Dewey, and Louie's Junior Woodchuck philosophy.

Even as a child, Eino was certain that he was one of the handful of souls chosen by Calvin and God for induction into Heaven, but how could Eino be certain in his certainty? He needed a sign from God. Maybe, he thought, if I become outstanding in some way, that will be the sign. He looked for a unique place for himself in the world. *What can I be that no one else has ever been?* he wondered.

After Eino graduated from the Lincoln Road Primary School, he worked in the woods with his grandfather. Occasionally, he was bothered by the knowledge that he had dropped out of school, but he was also quite certain that he already knew all that was worth knowing. He knew, for example, that the universe was static and that God was at the center of it. He knew that God was behind every single action, that God was good, and that the universe was ultimately logical. He considered himself an intelligent person and was certain that he would have no trouble understanding the logic of the universe.

One afternoon in the woods, Eino was limbing trees and listening secretly to music on a portable radio. He heard a piece of music worthy of Väinämöinen—a piece of music with magical qualities. The song was about a dog, but Eino knew instantly that the song could cause women to tear their hair, cry out in ecstasy, and rip off their clothes. That weekend, Eino got a ride into Coppertown and went looking for the music. "I'm looking for a song about a dog," Eino told the clerk in the music store. "Väinämöinen would have loved the song," Eino explained, but the clerk, whose last name was Wisniewski, had never heard of the *Kalevala*. He let Eino listen to renditions of "Old Shep" and "How

Much is That Doggie in the Window?" but Eino rejected them. Eventually, by going one by one through the hit songs of the day, Eino found the song and bought a copy. He also bought a small portable record player and took both home to the farm.

That evening, Eino played the magical song for Aili, and she hated it. One part of her wanted to snap the record in half and throw the pieces in the trash, but the other part realized that the song was only about a dog and, therefore, harmless. Eino told her the song was "Hound Dog" by somebody named Elvis. "If Väinämöinen were alive today, he'd play the guitar and sing like this guy," Eino told his mother.

A month later, Eino bought himself a Gibson guitar and a scarlet cowboy shirt with a three-inch white fringe on the sleeves and with an arrow design on the pockets. Every evening after work, he wore his new shirt and practiced guitar chords and sang incantations from the *Kalevala* while yearning always to be recognized as the modern Väinämöinen. Eino sang about putting his enemy "waist-deep in the swamp beneath him,/Hip-deep in the marshy meadow,/To his arm-pits in a quicksand." Eino wondered if one day he, too, like Elvis, would have a hit record. "If Elvis can make it with a song about a dog, I should be able to make it with a song about a swamp," he told Aili

After Eino grew up, he stopped going to church. He told Aili that he already knew about God's truth, so he didn't need somebody else explaining it to him every week. Eino began to spend a lot of his off-hours in a local bar where the proprietor let him play his guitar for the clientele. Eino's cowboy shirt became his trademark as an entertainer. He also always wore an ancient pitch-stained red baseball cap that advertised a brand of a chainsaw on the visor.

Eino soon discovered that he knew a lot more about the world than many of the bar's regular customers. Most of them had not had any contact with a book since their mothers read them *The Little Engine That Could* when they were toddlers. Eino tried to teach them the logical way the world worked. Eino explained how God had created the world by dividing the waters. "It's all in *Genesis*," he told them. One of the regulars at the bar was a some-time tradesman's helper named Jakko. Jakko, who had a history of difficult relationships with women, often stayed in the bar until it closed. After a couple of Old Milwaukees, he sometimes liked to argue, and this time he chose to scoff at Eino's theology, but Eino proved the truth of his argument beyond any doubt. "It rains everywhere in the world at one time or another," said Eino. "Even in the driest desert, it rains sometimes." Jakko had to admit that Eino was right so far. "That means there's a heck of a lot of water up there in the heavens and all around us. That's what you'd get if God divided the waters to make the world."

Jakko still questioned Eino's logic. "Then why doesn't all that water fall on our heads and drown us?" he said.

Eino explained that the sky was a kind of roof. "The world is hundreds of years old," said Eino. "Maybe even a thousand. So here and there the roof keeps springing leaks. Probably there are hundreds of angel roofers with tar buckets up there constantly patching new leaks."

"So why didn't God make a perfect roof that wouldn't leak?" asked Jakko, still confused.

"Because we need the rain," said Eino. "God made a roof that is imperfectly perfect. It leaks just the right amount."

Jakko couldn't argue with that kind of logic, and soon Eino had a reputation among the bar crowd as some kind of genius. "Eino could think his way through drywall," said Waino, another regular who worked odd jobs with a variety of local carpenters.

Eino's years passed—most of them uneventful. Eino's days followed one another with the same monotonous patterns repeated again and again. Every morning except Sunday, the grandparents, Eino, and Aili rose at five. The grandmother prepared a large pot of oatmeal for breakfast while the others got ready for work. After breakfast, Aili drove to her job in Coppertown, and Eino and his grandfather drove into the woods to drop trees, limb them, sometimes peel them, drag them by horse or tractor to the load site, cut them into mill lengths, load them onto the truck bed and take them to the mill.

Eventually, the grandfather retired, and Eino went into the woods alone. In 1965, the grandparents died a month apart. Aili inherited the farm, and she and Eino continued to live there. In 1975, Aili discovered that she had pancreatic cancer, and, a few months later, she too was gone.

Eino had her name and dates printed on a polished pink granite tombstone, and underneath he had them write SHE KEPT A CLEAN HOUSE. Now Eino was alone with a large bank account. He bought himself his first TV, for companionship. He still yearned to make something special of himself. Eino considered himself a rather sophisticated person who ought to be creating a memorable life. He mentioned his sophistication in the bar he frequented. Another patron, Sulo Partanen, found that idea to be incredibly funny. He looked at Eino, with his dirty and threadbare jeans and flannel shirt, and Sulo began to laugh. "Tell me about your sophistication," Sulo told Eino.

"I know there are special times when I should buy my Old Milwaukee in bottles instead of in cans," Eino explained. "I know there are times when spaghetti sauce requires fresh mushrooms, so I should open the can of mushrooms on the same day I make the sauce. I know that a can of black pepper poured into a radiator will seal a small leak," he added. "Jalapeños will not do the trick."

"And what vocation should Eino the Sophisticate have?" asked Sulo, who was on his eighth can of Old Milwaukee and who hated Eino's pretensions a little bit more with each minute that passed.

"I'd like to be recognized as a prophet," said Eino.

Sulo almost choked on his beer. "The only prophets in the Copper Country are bartenders," he said.

Right then Eino knew what he had to do. He quit the woods, withdrew his life savings from Superior National Bank, and soon bought himself a bar that had just come up for sale in Coppertown. He named it the First Finnish Lutheran Bar of the Copper Country in order to keep out clientele he considered riffraff, such as Catholics, Baptists, and Methodists. Eino spent days trying to think of an appropriate Finnish saying to have carved in the wood above the bar. He finally came up with something that he considered profound: THERE ARE FOUR KINDS OF PEOPLE IN THE WORLD— THOSE WHO HAVE READ THE *KALEVALA*, THOSE WHO WILL READ IT, THOSE WHO WILL NEVER READ IT, AND THOSE WHO HAVE SEEN THE MOVIE.

At the grand opening, Jakko was one of Eino's first customers. Jakko read the profundity over the bar and then insisted that Hollywood had never made the *Kalevala* into a movie.

Eino had never thought of that possibility and did not want to pay to have the carved words redone. He also didn't want to look like a fool, so he decided to bluff his way through the argument. "Sure they did," he told Jakko. "Way back in the old days."

"Then who played Väinämöinen?" Jakko asked.

"Humphrey Bogart," said Eino.

Jakko knew Eino was lying, but Jakko had never used a library card catalogue—in fact, he had never used a library at all—and, therefore, didn't know how to check on Eino's facts. For a moment, Jakko wondered what to do. Then he, too, decided to bluff his way through the argument. "You're right," he said. "I saw the film years ago on late-night TV. Barbara Stanwyck played the wicked witch of the north."

Eino's bar specialized in Copper Country Happy Meals—a pickled egg and a draft of Old Milwaukee. He also advertised a Bloody Toivo, which was an Old Milwaukee mixed with tomato juice and served with a sprig of dill.

Eino met his future wife in the bar in January 1983. Aino was no maiden by any definition. The last of her five children had already finished high school and was out in the world working. She had just divorced her abusive and alcoholic husband after twenty years of hellish marriage. At the bar, she liked to tell her life story over and over again to whoever would listen. Soon, all the regulars knew that Aino had had a long series of boyfriends in her youth, had had several bouts with alcoholism, and had had frequent forays with boredom. Then she had married a man who had beaten her up at least once a month. Now she was on her own, was bored, and was seeking another husband. Eventually, she chose Eino as the potential man of her dreams, but she was up front with him. "I need a man who will give me security," she said through her false teeth, her stringy blonde hair falling over her left eye in a manner that she considered seductive. "You have a house and property, a business, a bank account, and a pickup truck."

"The bank account is small," said Eino. "Almost all of my money is tied up in this bar."

"But a bar is the steadiest job in the Upper Peninsula," Aino answered. "I also want a man in my bed. I like sex. If I don't have sex periodically, I get tense and can't sleep."

Eino was willing to help her sleep soundly, and, a year later, they got married. They had little in common, but that didn't seem to matter. Eino's life changed little. He still rose at the same hour and spent the same number of hours as the proprietor of the bar. It quickly became obvious to him, however, that Aino had been a good investment. She couldn't stand the drabness of the inside of the farmhouse and quickly began a transformation of rooms that had not been renovated for fifty or more years. She ripped out sagging walls, put up new drywall, mudded, papered, painted. She revarnished floors and hired Aino's friend Waino to replace some windows and to patch a leak. She bought knickknack shelves and pictures and decorated the walls. She even tried to throw out the Formica table, but Eino would not hear of it. "You can change the rest of the house," he said, "but leave the kitchen and the living room alone. Those rooms represent my history."

Eino discovered that Aino had other passions besides keeping her house clean and bright. She liked to drink Miller Lite and to play Bingo. In the second year of their marriage, she bought herself a computer and liked to spend hours banging away on its keys. Eventually, she linked her machine up to something called the Internet. Eino never went near the machine and considered it some kind of infernal and treacherous thing invented by the devil himself. When Aino was not banging away on the computer keys, she frequently went out with girlfriends to drink and to play Bingo—sometimes at one of the women's homes and sometimes at the new casino that had opened in Baraga. Often she was still out when Eino came home exhausted from the bar. When Aino finally came home, she often woke him for sex. "Let's have a quick one," she'd say. Afterwards, she would sleep deeply, her teeth in a glass on the bedstand, while Eino lay awake watching her snore and thinking how lucky he was to have a woman like Aino in his bed after all of his years of bachelorhood.

Eino's life began to change the day in 1996 when a Michigan Tech graduate student in mathematics came into the bar to have a drink and conversation with the locals. The student was a specialist in something called pure research at MTU. He had been working for several years on indecipherable problems in irrational numbers, Eino had never heard of irrational numbers and didn't think such things were possible. Eino had figured out how to measure the cords in a truckload of wood, but, beyond that, he had never thought about math. He didn't even bother to balance his checkbook since the bank did it for him every month, and, as long as there was money in the bar's till, he didn't worry about profits from his business either.

The graduate student seemed to enjoy Eino's curiosity about irrational numbers. He told Eino about square roots and used four and sixteen as examples. Then he asked Eino to give him the square root of two, and Eino couldn't do it. The student laughed and said the number was irrational. Then the student told Eino about pi. "The number just goes on and on forever," said the student gleefully. Eino was horrified. He knew that anything that was irrational made no sense, and everything had to make sense because it was part of God's plan. His mother had taught him that. "How can irrational numbers exist in God's world?" Eino asked the student.

The student said that he didn't know but that they just did. Eino became suddenly afraid. If numbers could be irrational, then what else made no sense? Were these strange and dangerous numbers a door into the universal chaos that Eino suspected all Finns always feared? Were they the signs and symbols of unknown, malevolent forces? Were they the devil at work? No. The devil was part of God's plan and, therefore, part of a logical system. These numbers were different from the devil.

Eino had not questioned the essential meaning of things since he finished the Lincoln Road Primary School nearly fifty years before. He had always found clear and unquestionable theological answers to all of life's questions based upon his interpretation of the Bible, of the teachings of the church founders, of *Uncle Arthur's Bedtime Bible Stories*. These sources had always held the key to existence, but now all was in doubt. Eino had no answer for the existence of irrational numbers.

Eino lost faith in everything.

That very night, his body failed him, and everything in his world began to collapse. At three A.M., Aino came home from Bingo, climbed naked into Eino's bed, and said she wanted a quick one. She waited for him to climb aboard, but nothing happened. When his faith in the logic of all things disappeared, his confidence disappeared, too. He was suddenly terrified. Sweat ran down his forehead. His manhood curled into a tiny ball and practically disappeared into his body.

Aino waited a few seconds, glared over at him, cleared her throat loudly in disgust and rolled away from him. Eino tried to tell her it was because of irrational numbers, but she wouldn't listen. "Go to sleep!" she ordered him. "You're old!" Then Aino promptly fell asleep, and Eino lay there all night—grief-stricken that life as he had known it was forever over.

Before dawn, Eino crept into the living room to watch TV. In a documentary, a Mafia hitman was describing the preferred way of dispatching a victim. "Place the barrel just behind his right ear," he said. "Angle the barrel slightly up and toward the front of the head. It works like a charm. You'll have a clean kill—no thrashing around and no groans. Instant death."

Eino sat on his grandmother's couch and tried to imagine what it would be like to shoot himself in the head, to blow his brains out through the top of his skull. Eino imagined the cool barrel of a .38 just behind his ear. The tip of the barrel would leave a small red ring along his hair line. Eino squeezed the trigger hundreds of times as he sat there, but each imaginary explosion did not make him feel any better. He still felt the void where his life force was supposed to be. He still felt a shrinking definition of who he was.

"I'm a man," he said to himself. "I've worked hard all my life, and for what?" The sound of his voice brought no relief because he no longer felt like a man. He felt only a numbness now. He felt dead—as if the dream gun at his temple had already fired but as if the bullet were still moving in slow motion down the barrel.

Over breakfast, Aino gave Eino an ultimatum. "I won't live in a sexless marriage," she said. "It's too stressful, and I've already had years of stress with my first husband. You're a good person, Eino, but I will want a divorce if you remain impotent."

Eino didn't know what to say. He wanted to explain that his impotence had nothing to do with her—that, in fact, he found her still wonderfully desirable—but he said nothing.

After breakfast, Aino disappeared upstairs. Eino could hear her rummaging around in her clothes closet, and he wondered what she was doing. *She's probably going to change something else around here*, he thought as he consumed a second cup of coffee. He stayed in the kitchen longer than usual, thinking about his mother. He had several more cups of coffee before he left for work.

Later, as Eino cleaned up the bar in preparation for its opening, Jakko came by and saw immediately that something was wrong. He badgered Eino until he got the whole story. "I don't see any problem here," said Jakko. "Those irrational numbers are part of God's plan, too."

Eino wanted to know how.

"It's the same as the problem of good and evil," explained Jakko. "Nobody would know what good was unless evil existed. You can only define what is good through its opposite. Therefore, evil has to exist in God's perfect world so that we can all learn to be good. If you're going to have the sense of two plus two equals four, then you have to have the nonsense of irrational numbers. Two plus two is part of this world. Irrational numbers are part of the anti-world."

Eino wasn't sure he agreed with any of Jakko's argument, but it still made him feel better. Plus, Jakko said he had a sure cure for Eino's impotence. "It's an old Finnish cure passed down from father to son since the world began," Jakko said. Jakko asked Eino for a bottle of vodka and some money. Eino got the bottle from behind the bar and gave Jakko five dollars from the till. "I'll be right back," said Jakko. "I have to buy you some garlic and dill."

Jakko returned in a few minutes and used a garlic press that he produced from somewhere to squeeze several dozen cloves of garlic into the vodka. Then he added a generous spray of fresh dill and told Eino to drink the whole thing. "Soon you'll feel like a hero of old," Jakko said. "You'll be like Lemminkainen of the *Kalevala*. You'll be passing your nights 'amid lively maidens,/Sporting with the lively maidens,/Toying with their unbound tresses.'"

Eino guzzled down the vodka, feeling it burn all the way down into his feet, and it wasn't long before he felt quite lusty. The vodka warmed his entire body, and the garlic thinned his blood and increased his desire. But the presence of the dill baffled him. "What's the dill for?" he asked Jakko.

"It's good for the soul," said Jakko.

Eino decided to go home right then and find Aino. "I'm ready to take her to bed," he told Jakko.

When Eino reached the farm, Aino was gone. So were some of her clothes and a suitcase. There was a letter on the kitchen table. In it, Aino explained that she had met a man from North Dakota over the Internet. They had been punching out messages to each other for the past month while Eino was busy elsewhere. The man had sent Aino an airplane ticket, and Aino had eloped alone to meet her new man at the airport in Bismarck. "You're a good person, but I need something else in my life now," Aino had written.

Eino felt terrible. He dug his guitar out of the closet where it usually rested and took it with him back to the bar. When he returned, a number of the regulars were already there. Jakko had taken it upon himself to serve them. Eino sat on the end stool and began to play a mournful tune, which he made up on the spot. Then he added mournful words and began to sing with great vigor. Maybe it was the vodka at work or maybe it was the loss of his love. Whatever the reason, Eino began to produce great music. The regulars listened in awe. "Wow! That's great stuff. You've never played this well before," one of them said.

Eino just smiled and continued to sing. *Only Väinämöinen would understand what is swelling in my heart*, thought Eino.

Letter from the Land of Wolves

DEAR MIKA,
I heard from your mother that you'll be retiring from the Navy in a few months. It doesn't seem like it's been that long since we graduated from Jeffers and you left for the big world. Maybe now you'll find time to come back for a visit.

My father's in real bad health. His arthritic knees look like cabbages, and his left hip joint is broken right through the socket. When he puts weight on it, the pain makes him cantankerous as hell. He creeps around on a crutch and swears a blue streak. I visit him at the farm pretty often and weed and till his garden. I also cut the grass and in winter plow his driveway.

Last fall, I set a rocking chair in the back field. Every day during hunting season, he sat there with his gun. The deer came out every day because we fed them old potatoes, apples, and carrots. Pa's practically blind, though, and he couldn't see them. Just before dark on the last day of the season, he noticed a lot of movement out by the feed. He squinted across the field for a long time and finally made out a big foraging buck. He missed it three times, but the buck just kept eating. The fourth shot dropped him. Pa says he missed because he was sitting awkwardly, but I think he missed in order to show me how well he had trained that deer. That buck never moved while Pa tested its patience.

This past weekend, my son and I drove to Agate Beach. Do you remember the little pool where the river enters into the lake? You and I used to have some good times there when we were boys. Five years ago, a couple of Toivola girls drowned there. I went out with the fire department when the alarm came in. We found both in a couple of minutes. It was August after a dry spell and the water was real shallow. A man could have crossed that pool's deepest part in three steps. It didn't matter. The Hietala girl couldn't swim, panicked, and pulled the Aho girl down. We had to leave them on the shore for the coroner. The bastard took a long time. I was sick for days afterwards, and I haven't fished the river since. My boy wanted to go swimming in that same spot, but I told him he'd have to walk home if he did.

Do you remember old Don Erkkila? He was already old when we were boys, so he must be eighty-five now. He's still logging with his chainsaw. He cuts all year round. In the winter, he drops the trees at snowline, and in the spring he cuts the stumps. A few years ago, he sent for a mail-order bride from Russia. She must have been all of eighteen when he brought her over. They got married, but since then she's been in the sack with every man who showed any interest. Old Don's always made money and has never spent any, so I suppose she's sticking around long enough for him to die. Trouble is, he just keeps going. He's a tough old fart.

The last time my boys and I saw old Don, we were out dirt biking and got lost. We heard Don's chainsaw. We asked him for directions out of the woods, but the straightest and easiest route would have taken us past his house, and I guess he figured my boys and I were prime candidates for more tomcatting, so he gave us the wrong directions. He almost killed us on a trail that hedged us between a ridge face and a swamp. Somewhere on that trail, we passed the headquarters of the Upper Peninsula Trappers' Association. The sign on the door said it all: DO-GOODERS AND LIBERALS KEEP OUT!

The cabin is owned by Kip Niemi. He used to be a devout Lutheran until the pastor crossed him. Then he sent away for a mail-order divinity degree from a California outfit and started his own church in the basement of a building supplies company. He suckered the congregation into building a real church and an adjacent school on the back road near Paavola. The people who teach there are so dumb that the name of the town is misspelled on the school's athletic jerseys. The coach's excuse is, "I ain't no Finn."

Old John Saari is dead. He carried a .45 on his hip all his life and boasted of shooting his enemies and burying them in a swamp. No one knew of anyone who was missing, so no one pressed charges.

We did have a bona fide murder a couple of years ago. A downstate fellow named O'Brien bought the Partanen place. He did a little farming on the side and worked in the sawmill. One of the Keranen boys started a feud with him over a Savela woman. Keranen already had a reputation for burning down barns in the middle of the night and threatened to do the same to O'Brien's. O'Brien went days and days not daring to sleep. One night in February, Keranen came to play poker with drinking buddies who rented a shack just a hundred feet beyond O'Brien's property line.

When O'Brien saw Keranen's parked car, he went berserk, burst
into the cabin, and blasted Keranen with a shotgun. Keranen
snapped upright, spilled the cards to the floor, took two steps, and
fell across the woodstove. Keranen's buddies tried to pull him off
the red-hot stove, but O'Brien shouted that they'd get the same if
they touched him. "Let the bastard fry!" O'Brien cried, and
Keranen did. They gave O'Brien two years for manslaughter, but
he's out on probation. I saw him the other day repairing his barn
roof. He seemed happy.

He's certainly happier than crazy Paavo Muttinen. You and
he used to shine deer. Remember? He's been through so many
episodes that no man could remember half of them. He lost his
beautiful first wife—the one that looked like an Indian princess.
She disappeared after she found out that he'd been visiting his best
friend's wife. Then Paavo became the county's top drug dealer.
After state cops busted one of his CAT labs, Paavo was put on trial,
but the judge disappeared. When a lawyer asked Paavo about the
disappearance, Paavo guessed that the judge might be in an old
mine shaft. Of course, there are dozens of abandoned shafts around
here, and most of them are flooded. They brought frogmen from all
over to search those old shafts, but they never found the judge.
Paavo used to go and watch the divers. He thought it was funny as
hell. A couple of years ago, Paavo remarried, but wife number two
began to run around with a car dealer. Paavo came home one night
to find the guy's car in his yard. Paavo smashed the windows with
a Louisville slugger, poured gasoline over the interior and lit it up.
What a waste of a brand-new car! A week later, Paavo burned the
dealer's garage and lot—cars, trucks, everything. Of course, there
was no proof. The salesman put out a contract on Paavo, but the
hitman (a regular in local bars) fled with the money to Ironwood for
a vacation. When the money ran out, the hitman asked for more.
The dealer was so angry that he told the cops he was being black-
mailed. Then the cops found out about the contract. The dealer
and the hitman were both given suspended sentences. Now Paavo
is suing the dealer for two million dollars for psychological stress.
Paavo has good lawyers from downstate. He figures his reputation
hasn't traveled that far yet.

Today I saw Henry Kujala. Do you remember how he used
to eat his school books before the teachers kicked him out? A real
nervous guy. He's made a good living lately by standing in the

middle of Route 41 with a cowboy hat and a toy badge and stopping tourists. He charges a dollar for using the road—says it's a toll.

I often go fishing with Phil Lokojarvi. He has a camp on Keweenaw Bay. Last winter, two runaways from the state farm broke into his cabin and stayed about two weeks. They burned every stick of his wood. He had about fifteen gallons of snowmobile fuel, which they used, too. They drove all over the lake until an ice fisherman informed Phil. The state cops came to the camp, but the boys hightailed it up the bay on Phil's snowmobile. They broke through the ice and drowned. Phil was mad as hell about the snowmobile. He'd only had it a year. This spring, we fished it out, but it doesn't run right.

Nothing else has happened around here—just the same old people doing the same old things. Hell, I don't even know half the people anymore. You were smart to get out. Guess you'll find something else interesting to do now that you're retired. Here life just goes on.

Bob

The Negaunee Order of *Suomi Kutsuu* Watchers

Lönnrot Is Reborn in Michigan

BILL PALOSAARI WAS A ROUGH, tough Negaunee iron worker from the day he quit school to the day he fell off a scaffold and shattered his legs all the way to his hips. During Bill's long and painful recuperation, he lay quietly in his bed and alternately drank coffee and Old Milwaukee. After the casts came off, something seemed to have gone out of Bill. He was no longer the loud and energetic man he had once been. In forced retirement, he seemed to have no spirit. Although he was only in his early fifties, he no longer had the energy to cook up the bacon and eggs that he loved for breakfast.

Instead, he now made a big vat of oatmeal about once a month and stuck it in the refrigerator for multiple breakfasts. Each morning, Bill scooped out a bowlful of the heavy, viscous stuff and heated it in the microwave. The texture was different from fresh oatmeal. Each bowlful had the graininess of underwatered wet cement. Bill could stand his spoon on end in the middle of the stuff, and the sugar and milk refused to blend.

Sometimes Bill rounded off breakfast with a little All-Bran and a cup of yesterday's leftover coffee. The coffee sometimes had mold floating on the top because Bill was too lazy ever to clean the pot. Bill was lazy with his All-Bran, too. He bought it in the little one-serving-size boxes. Each morning, he took one box out of the case stashed under the sink between the unused Brillo pads and the dishwashing liquid. He ripped open the front of the box and its wax-lined inner package. Then he poured in the milk and spooned the bran right from the box. That way, he only had to rinse the spoon when he was done.

As Bill got lazier, he frequently slipped into catatonic states for hours at a time. Bill became especially catatonic while watching TV. His ultimate catatonic state was reached when he gathered with his friends on Sunday morning to watch *Suomi Kutsuu* (*Finland Calling*) from Channel Six in Marquette. His friends misunderstood Bill's hypnotic state. Because he was sitting with his eyes wide open and his body absolutely stationary, they assumed that he was extremely interested in the show. Actually, Bill didn't even know the TV was on.

Bill's friends nominated and then elected him to the position of Chief Monk of the Negaunee Order of *Suomi Kutsuu* Watchers. Each Sunday without fail, Bill and a couple of dozen of his iron worker buddies gathered at Bill's house to watch *Suomi Kutsuu*. The gathering was in lieu of church for all the guys, and the show's host, Carl Pellonpaa, was a kind of Lord High Wizard of the Airways for the iron workers. Carl had more authority than the union boss because he was the voice of the Old Country. Whenever Carl talked to an especially excited troupe of Finnish entertainers, the iron workers took note of his words and repeated them endlessly through the remainder of the week. "And how long have you been the director of the Association of Dental Assistants in Finland?" one of the iron workers might blurt out on a Tuesday evening while the gang sat in and around a booth at a local bar.

"Carl asked that question last year on the same show in which he interviewed the businessman from Helsinki who sold Finnish gum in the pharmacies of the Upper Peninsula," someone else might answer. "It was just after the Finnish hymns played on an accordion by that old fart from Aura."

"You got it!" the first speaker would say, and the others would give each other knowing looks. Rarely was the group stumped by a question about *Finland Calling*, and, if they were, they reviewed the video tapes and refreshed their memories of Finnish culture.

On Sunday morning, just as *Suomi Kutsuu* was about to begin, Bill Palosaari's catatonic state increased by half a notch, and, instead of simply withdrawing psychically from the world, Bill died. The gang debated for a while what they ought to do. In the end, they watched *Suomi Kutsuu* straight through without doing anything. "Bill would have wanted it this way," they said as justification for their inaction. Then one of them called an ambulance, and they all waited around until Bill's body was carted away by the boys in white.

The iron workers were shocked to learn that Bill had had enough foresight to write a will. They were even more shocked to learn that he had left his house and considerable savings to the Negaunee Order of *Suomi Kutsuu* Watchers. In the will, which was read to the assembled Watchers in Bill's lawyer's office, Bill left the Order over three hundred thousand dollars. The money was part of the $750,000 settlement Bill had gotten for his shattered legs. In the will, Bill urged the Watchers to get a new big-screen TV with some of the money and to treat his home like the Order's temple. "In case you're wondering," Bill added at the end of the will, "I've been reincarnated in Finland."

"What do you suppose that last part means?" asked one of the iron workers.

"It means he's been reborn in the Old Country as a Finnish kid," said another iron worker.

"And what does that mean?" asked a third.

"It means it's a call for action," said a fourth. "Since Bill died, the Negaunee Order of *Suomi Kutsuu* Watchers lacks a chief monk. What good is a temple without a spiritual leader? Sure, we have Carl Pellonpaa, but we need an interpreter of Carl's scripture. We have to send a delegation to Finland to find Bill's reincarnation and bring him back here as a kind of king of Negaunee's spiritual life."

One of the iron workers contacted a Marquette travel agency, and soon the Negaunee Order of Suomi Kutsuu Watchers had chartered a FinnAir flight to Helsinki. In order to look good for the folks in Finland, the entire Order traipsed to Kmart and bought new flannel shirts and jeans. One member bought a fresh bottle of Canoe cologne so they'd smell good, too.

The flight to Finland was uneventful. None of the iron workers had ever flown, and all were nervous, but, by mid-Atlantic, they had consumed forty-two dozen miniature bottles of airline booze and felt just fine. They weren't sure how they would find the reincarnation of Bill once they got to Helsinki, but they had brought along a poster of Carl Pellonpaa because they figured that might help. Across the poster one of the iron workers had written BE ALL YOU CAN BE with a magic marker.

In the hotel in Helsinki, the iron workers ate and drank and wondered what to do. They had already discovered that their Negaunee version of Finnish caused Finns to break into gales of laughter. In the same hotel was an English-speaking refugee from Namibia who was in Finland on a tourist visa while she looked for the father of her illegitimate child, a cute four-year-old boy. The errant father had been a social worker with a Finnish missionary society in Namibia, and he had gotten a bit too cozy with the Namibian woman.

While the iron workers were having breakfast one morning, the four-year-old half Nambian/half Finn wandered over to their table. The little boy's mother had run out of money the day before and had no means to buy the boy breakfast. The little boy was hungry. The poster of Carl Pellonpaa lay on the floor by the iron workers' table. The boy picked up the poster and began to gnaw on a corner of the picture. The iron workers took this as a sign. "This kid must be Bill's reincarnation," one of them said. "He finds *Suomi Kutsuu* as tasteful as we do."

"He don't look like Bill," said another iron worker. "He don't even look like a Finn!"

The Namibian woman had to return to Africa the next day because her visa was up. At home, she had no way of supporting her half-white child, and her family had expelled her for her indiscretion. After the iron workers explained the purpose of their mission, she gave them the child. "We'll have him call you each Christmas," they promised, "and you can visit Negaunee any time you wish." The following day, the iron workers flew back to Michigan with the child monk.

They named the boy Bill Palosaari Junior and set out to teach him the tenets of their Order. As a group, they taught the boy to curse in two languages. They taught him the importance of iron workers and the unimportance of bankers and insurance agents. They taught him disdain for scab workers. They taught him to make wood, pank snow, and drink black coffee. They dressed him in flannel shirts, jeans, and baseball caps and with reverence placed swampers on his feet. They taught him a love of the NRA and a hatred of the DNR. Every Sunday, they sat him on a cushion in front of the big-screen TV and forced him to watch *Suomi Kutsuu*. When he was little and wanted to run around instead, they held him in their laps, set the TV directly in front of him, and turned up the volume. After each show, they questioned him about what he had seen. At night, in place of bedtime stories, they gave the boy a biographical sketch of Carl Pellonpaa's life—how Carl had once been a pretty good baseball player who had had a tryout with the Boston Braves and how Carl had once been a ski jumper, though not in the same class with the Bietila brothers. "Carl is a remarkable guy," they told him. "That's why he's Master of Ceremonies on *Suomi Kutsuu*."

For Christmas, the iron workers gave the child a shovel with a red ribbon on the handle and told him it was a manual snow blower. They gave him a Radio Flyer and told him it was a manual pickup truck. They gave him an ax and told him it was a manual chainsaw.

Bill Palosaari Junior grew up to be very peculiar, even for Negaunee. He left school in his sophomore year and spent his days listening to *Talk Hate* radio. He especially liked Rush Limbaugh's show but was terrified that the virulent messages would leak radioborne pathogens into the air he breathed. All day he hovered close to the radio while dressed in gloves, a gown, a face shield, eye protection, a mouthpiece, and a ventilation device. There was no way his skin or mucus membrane were going to come in contact with contaminated air.

Bill Junior had a missionary's zeal for teaching the truth of *Suomi Kutsuu* to nonbelievers. Some of Bill Senior's money was still in the bank. Bill Junior withdrew most of it and had thousands of videotaped copies made of old *Suomi Kutsuu* shows. He planned to distribute the tapes to the masses. He saw himself as a modern version of Elias Lönnrot, who compiled the national epic of the Finns, "I am compiling the epic of the Upper Peninsula," he told the iron workers. "I hope to have copies of every *Suomi Kutsuu* show, from its inception to the present, in the video tape collections of everyone throughout the world by the end of the century."

At first, Bill Junior passed out free tapes on street corners, in bars, and at snowmobile trail crossings from Sault St. Marie to Ironwood. Whenever someone came by, Bill Junior thrust a tape in his hand and urged him to watch it as soon as possible. "If you like what you see and want the entire collection, just call me at this number," he would tell potential *Suomi Kutsuu*-ites, and he'd give the person his card. The card read BILL PALOSAARI JUNIOR, CHIEF MONK, NEGAUNEE ORDER *SUOMI KUTSUU* WATCHERS. The card included Bill Junior's phone number.

No one ever called.

Bill Junior advertised the tapes in newspapers and magazines from Maine to California. Still, no one ordered and no one called.

In disgust, Bill Junior decided to go on a spiritual quest to the Westwood Mall in Marquette. He bought a couple of new shirts in the mall's Kmart and then walked around for a while, searching for answers. *Maybe I should go to the Copper Country*, he thought. *There are a heck of a lot of Finns up there, and maybe they can give me some spiritual direction.* Then Bill Junior remembered that the

Finnish guests on *Suomi Kutsuu* were sometimes from Minnesota, where there were also lots of Finns. Bill Junior had never been out of the Upper Peninsula since his arrival from Finland at the age of four, and the whole idea of traveling as far as Minnesota made him nervous, but, in the end, he was determined to go. *After all*, he thought, *people over there are named Eino, too.*

Bill Junior traveled by bus to Minneapolis, taking with him a coat, a few changes of clothes and a sleeping bag in a back pack, a sack of preservable foods in a cooking pot, and a big roll of bills in large denominations. He thought about taking an ax and a shovel but didn't. He also debated about taking along a big box of *Suomi Kutsuu* tapes to distribute but decided against it. He didn't want the disappointment if people refused them, and the purpose of the trip was to give his life direction.

Outside the Minneapolis bus station, Bill Junior was mugged by a three-hundred-pound Hmong who held Bill Junior upside down in order to shake the roll of bills out of his pocket. The Hmong thanked Bill Junior for making such a large donation to the welfare of the Hmong's family, and then the Hmong walked away, leaving Bill penniless.

Bill could not afford to stay anywhere, and the crowds frightened him. He wandered across the city without speaking to anyone. Eventually, he came to a bridge crossing the Mississippi River. The water ran very fast, and its soft, sibilant roar soothed Bill Junior's shattered nerves. For a long time, he stood at the south rail staring at the water and ignoring the steady flow of pedestrian and automobile traffic. Soon night fell, and only a few cars and an occasional pedestrian still crossed the bridge.

A few hours later, all human traffic ceased, and only the eternal dark waters flowed ceaselessly. Bill Junior could no longer see the water but could hear its strength, its elastic energy. It seemed to be alive. Bill curled up against the bridge rail and let himself be lulled to sleep.

In the morning, he ate several strips of beef jerky and a raw potato. After breakfast, he took a long rope from his pack, tied it to his cooking pot and lowered the pot into the river. The water tugged powerfully against Bill's arms and shoulders, and he could feel the river's life. Hand over hand, he drew up the pot, now full of cool river water. Bill lifted the can over the railing and set it close against the base of the railing, out of the path of pedestrians. For the remainder of the day, whenever Bill needed to be rejuvenated, he drank from the pot, the cool water glistening as it slipped rhapsodically down his throat and into his stomach.

All that day, Bill sat or stood by the railing and watched the water flow. No one bothered him. Bill felt that he had found a place to stay. Several people handed Bill small coins as they passed, but most ignored him. Bill gave the first coin to the river as an offering, but he pocketed the others. In the early evening, Bill walked to a store and bought a large bag of chips, a box of Little Debbies, and a Twinkie. He returned to the bridge to eat and threw the trash over the railing into the river.

Bill sat or stood by the bridge rail for many days. He wasn't sure exactly how long he had been there. He lost track of time. *Why should I keep track of the minutes?* Bill wondered. *The river has no time. Or maybe it has all the time. It just flows and I watch it flow.*

A few days later, a man hello-ed Bill from the top window of a nearby skyscraper. The man's voice carried the same kind of urgent message as the river, so Bill looked up. He could just see the man as a dark patch against the flat gray wall of the building's upper story. The man was waving, so Bill waved back. That wave was Bill's first real contact with anyone in Minneapolis. Bill's heart pounded painfully from fright, but he continued bravely to wave.

Then the man jumped, his body arching angelically outward toward the river. It was safe for Bill to return the wave when the man was far away, but now he was rushing toward Bill at a terrible speed, and Bill didn't know what to do. All the way down, the man kept waving, and Bill, frozen by the knowledge that he would soon have to make contact with this falling angel, stupidly returned the wave. Bill thought the man intended to land on the bridge, but he did not. He sailed past Bill with a smile on his face and with his right arm still extended in a wave. Bill still waved back and continued to wave as the man shot toward the river. Bill leaned out over the railing in time to see that the man had tilted his face in Bill's direction and was still watching Bill as he struck the water. There was no sound from the impact, and the water, intent only upon rushing to the sea, did not seem to be disturbed at all by the man's arrival.

Bill watched for a long time to see if a head or an arm would disturb the surface, but neither did. After that, Bill forgot about the man and just watched the water, but soon a diving team arrived from somewhere, and the river was disturbed by boats and divers and grappling hooks. A policeman came onto the bridge and joined Bill at the railing. "Did you see the poor bastard go into the water?" he asked Bill. Bill said that he had. The policeman asked Bill to point out exactly where the body had struck the surface. Bill told him and pointed. Then the policeman shouted commands down to the men on the river.

"Who was he?" Bill asked.

"Just another disturbed Vietnam vet," said the policeman. "His wife says he was screwed up ever since he came home from the war. She was with him just before he jumped. She says he saluted all the way down. Is that true?"

"I thought he was waving to me," said Bill.

The policeman didn't say anything.

After the policeman and the divers left, Bill continued to stand at the railing. They hadn't found the body. Bill asked several passers-by if they had seen the man jump, but no one replied. Finally, Bill asked a small old woman if she had seen the man. "He jumped from up there," Bill said, pointing to the top of the building.

"This is a clean and orderly city," the old woman replied brusquely. "If you're thinking of suicide, forget it. If you had a job and a decent set of clothes, you wouldn't have time to think about such things. If you can't find anything else to do, join the Army. They'll make a man of you. They'll teach you to be all you can be." The old lady hurried away.

Bill thought of what she had said. Her parting words rang in his head. The iron workers had told Bill many times how he had been found. The story was part of the mythology of the Negaunee Order of *Suomi Kutsuu* Watchers. He now recalled the poster he had gnawed on in the restaurant in Helsinki. The poster had said BE ALL YOU CAN BE. The words were surely a sign. Plus the suicidist had been a soldier.

Bill now knew what he had to do. He abandoned his few possessions on the bridge and walked away to find meaning in life through an Army recruiting station.

As he walked, Bill pondered the ramifications of his decision. He might never return to Negaunee. If he didn't, would the Order survive? Of course it would, he realized. One man did not an Order make—not even its Chief Monk. *The Negaunee Order of* Suomi Kutsuu *Watchers will surely go on forever,* Bill thought. And they shall dwell in the house of Bill.

Erkki from Ahti Lemminkäinen
ᚯ ᚯ

Seeking a Comely Maiden from the North

GROWING UP ON THE FAMILY FARM near Vaasa in western Finland, Matti dreamed often of running away to Lapland, the land of wolves. As a boy, he read the *Kalevala* over and over and longed to emulate one of its heroes, Ahti Lemminkäinen, who journeyed far to the north in pursuit of an elk and a swan so he could win the love of "a comely Lapp maiden." But as a young man, the longest journey Matti ever made was across the farmyard in the winter of 1898 in order to reach the bed of the hired girl. Loviisa excited Matti because she too was Lapp, with coppery skin, coal-black hair, a flat nose, and the Mongolian folds of her ancestors. For Matti, Loviisa represented adventure, but, by spring, she was pregnant and insisted that he and she marry. Suddenly Matti saw himself tied down in an endless life of toil. What should he do? His boyhood friends had already fled to America to work in mines in Michigan. They described Hancock, Michigan, as a kind of magic kingdom. They wrote that anyone could become wealthy there if he was frugal and was willing to work hard. "You will have more money than you thought possible," one of them wrote to Matti. "And you will be among your own kind. Hancock is the center of Finnish culture in America. There's no place like it."

Matti hated the idea of being underground in a mine all day, but all that money was attractive. For a while, Matti debated abandoning Loviisa because his friends had abandoned their girl-friends, but, in the end, he sold his share of the farm to his brother, married Loviisa, and booked passage for both of them on a ship bound for New York.

On the ship, Matti became friendly with a Red Finn who was a wanted man in Finland. The czar's police had an invitation for the man—a free vacation in Siberia for an undefined length of time. "When they tried to give me the invitation," the Red Finn told Matti, "I fled across the soft spring ice of our lake and through a swamp. They were afraid to follow. They may be looking for me in America, too, so I'm going to get lost when I get there."

71

"But I thought all Finns in America were supposed to live in Michigan or Minnesota," said Matti.

"That's true for most of them," said the Red. "But there are also Finns in Brooklyn, Massachusetts, and Ohio. There are even a few in the distant West. I'm going to go where few Finns have gone before."

Matti wanted to know where that might be. "I don't know," said the Red. "I just want an adventure."

Matti liked that idea. The Red said he wanted a place as wild and uncivilized as Lapland. Matti and the Red borrowed a map of the United States from a ship's crewman and looked it over. In Finland, the Red had read a Swedish-language magazine that included stories about cowboys and Indians and, at the end of each story, somebody was killed in a gunfight. The Red decided to go to Tombstone in the Arizona Territory. "I want to be the first Finnish Socialist gunslinger in American history," he told Matti.

Before the ship reached New York, Matti spent a lot of time talking with Loviisa about the wonders of Hancock, Michigan, their future home. "My friends tell me that it is more impressive than Helsinki," he told her. "We're going to have a wonderful adventure there." Loviisa said nothing. She was large with child and the rocking of the ship often made her nauseated. She vomited several times a day and couldn't eat. She missed Lapland terribly. She hoped that Michigan would have great, flat open spaces and plenty of reindeer. "Is it a land of magic, like my homeland?" she asked Matti.

Every day, Matti practiced English phrases with the Red, but he didn't get far. The strange-sounding words got all tangled up on his tongue. Loviisa refused to learn any of the new language. "I am a *Sami*," she said. "I will speak only the language of my ancestors and the Finnish of my husband." Loviisa told the Finnish women on the ship how much she longed to be back in Lapland. The women were carrying their prejudice against Lapps with them to the New World, so they only smiled and said little to her. They left her out of most of their conversations. Among themselves, they said that they wished she was back in Lapland, too. "You don't even fit in on this ship," one of them told her. "How will you ever fit in when you get to America."

"Maybe you can live with Indians," said another. "They're nomadic, too."

In New York, one of the customs men tried to be friendly with Matti. "Three hundred thousand Finns like you have already gone through Ellis Island," he told Matti. "Most went to Michigan's Copper Country or Minnesota's Iron Range." The man was speaking English. Matti nodded but understood nothing. "Are you going to Michigan or Minnesota?" the man asked.

Matti, frightened, could remember only one word of his English phrases. "Yes," he said.

"Which state?" the customs man asked.

"Yes," said Matti.

"You're not very intelligent, are you?" said the man.

"Yes," said Matti.

Loviisa listened uncomprehendingly. "I hope they have tundra in Michigan," she said.

The customs man had no idea what she had said, but the strange words sounded guttural and harsh. "Did she just curse me?" he asked Matti.

The customs man pulled Matti and Loviisa out of the line and told them to stand to the side, along with a couple of other Finnish families. Then he indicated that they should go with a man who led them away. Unbeknownst to Matti and the others, the man was a recruiter for a mining company in northern Maine. Matti was no longer on his way to Hancock. He was now on his way to mine slate for the Portland-Monson Slate Company in Monson, Maine. The recruiter had paid the customs man to get him some strong young men who wouldn't cause trouble.

From Ellis Island, Matti and Loviisa could see the skyline of New York, but once they left the island with the recruiter and traveled to the train station, they got a full sense of the size of the city. "Wow!" exclaimed Matti. "Just look at this place! And we're only on the edge of America—hardly in the country. Imagine what Hancock must look like!"

Matti and Loviisa discovered on the train that other Finns were also going to New England destinations, but most of those others had sense enough to stop in Finnish communities in Fitchburg, Massachusetts, or in southern New Hampshire. One family traveled across the Maine border to the community of South Paris. Matti, however, had faith in the recruiter, who seemed friendly enough and who had bought Matti and Loviisa some food during a long layover in Boston. Therefore, Matti and his wife kept right on going until they reached the obscure hamlet of Monson on the fringe of civilization in north-central Maine. There they joined a handful of other Finns and Swedes who had been duped into going there to mine slate.

Monson, just south of Moosehead Lake, sat on the southern edge of Maine's empty quarter—a three-million-acre forest leased to large paper companies and containing virtually no population. Just south of the town, the train passed moose horns stuck on a post. The horns had been there since 1817 as a kind of symbol of the place. Loviisa mistook the horns for a reindeer rack and felt a sudden surge of hope. "Maybe it will be okay here after all," she told her husband.

For the final few miles of their journey through the forest, Matti and Loviisa rode on a narrow-gauge toy-sized train with a miniature engine and miniature cars. The mini-train was used by the slate company to move their goods from the pitheads to the actual railhead south of the town. The town itself was minute. It sat at the foot of Lake Hebron, surrounded by forest. The few businesses extended on slate pilings over water. The businesses were old and had fake square fronts like a Hollywood movie set of the Old West. None of the businesses were in good shape. They all had peeling paint, sagging roofs, and sinking foundations. There was a hotel, a barber shop, several grocery stores, a hardware store, a general store, a blacksmith shop, a combination garage and stable, and a machine shop.

The town had only about nine hundred people and appeared to be slowly dying. The high school on a knoll at the north end of town reflected that. The local school had real slate boards. The town's sidewalks were slate slabs. Most homes had slate walkways and slate steps. Wells had slate curbstones. Houses had slate shingles. Kitchens had slate sinks. Living rooms had slate lamps, and recreation rooms had slate pool tables. The town's dump was an unused slate pit. The garbage was dropped several hundred feet down a sheer drop-off to the waiting rats. Slate was the town's livelihood, its life. Slate was the tombstones that marked the townsfolk after slate had killed them in the pits.

The day after his arrival, Matti asked a Monson Finn what life was like in the town. "The winters are really long," the man said. "It's bitterly cold with temperatures of forty below zero in January."

"Thank God!" exclaimed Matti. "I was afraid it might be too warm." The man explained that spring always arrived late—at the beginning of summer—just like in Finland. "The summers are brief but beautiful," the man said. "There are a lot of long, cool days that fade slowly into evenings full of loon calls and brush strokes of wind through the trees."

"And what about the fall?" asked Matti.

"You get a lot of color in September, but then the leaves fall and you get a sort of dead brown landscape for weeks."

"Thank God!" said Matti. "So it's much like home."

Matti went to work in the pits immediately. He and Loviisa boarded at the hotel while they looked for a place of their own. Soon, with the last of their savings, they bought a rock-strewn piece of land three miles north of town. They cleared it and over a year's time built a home modeled on a Finnish farmstead, with adjoining sheds, a sauna, and a barn. Matti and Loviisa's first child, a daughter, was born before they moved in. Once they were ensconced on the farm, they bought a couple of pigs, some lambs, some bantam hens, and a cow. They cultivated a large garden.

Matti joined the Finnish Farmers' Union. The union had a clubhouse south of the town where they held dances on Saturday nights. Matti enjoyed the dances although he never danced. He and most of the other men hung outside in the parking lot, talking about work, eating snacks, and drinking a mixture of vodka and beer. Inside, the women whirled around and around the dance floor to the polka music of Jorma Raisanen.

Loviisa often stayed home, intentionally avoiding the festivities. When she did attend, the other women usually ignored her. Sometimes they would whisper small cruelties about her—even when she was present. They made fun of her Asiatic hair, the way she dressed, even the way she occasionally clung to Matti as if he could defend her from their jibes. At home in a trunk at the foot of her bed, she still had a traditional Lapp outfit, including a tall embroidered hat in layers of bright blue, yellow and red cloth. She also had warm Lapp boots covered with reindeer fur. The boots had curled-up, pointed toes decorated with balls of blue leather. Sometimes Loviisa dressed in these traditional clothes and then, alone in her bedroom, she wailed out her grief and her longing for home.

In one of the sheds, she distilled rich alcoholic beverages from chokecherries and raspberries, following a formula she remembered from her youth, when cloudberries were distilled into a powerful liquor by her parents in Lapland. Often when Matti came home from the dance, his body giving off the heavy fumes of vodka, Loviisa would greet him with a glass of homemade brandy in her hand. For the rest of the night, Matti would curse the slate pits, telling his wife again and again how much he hated the work. Loviisa would counter with how much she hated America. "I will never learn their cursed language," she would proclaim. "My heart is forever on the tundra."

Years passed. Matti and Loviisa had six children. While the children were still small, Matti fell from a derrick, landing on a slab of slate and smacking his head so hard that he became permanently deaf in his left ear. He also broke several bones and was laid up for months. The family struggled to survive with help from the Finnish Farmers' Union and the slate company. Then, less than a year after Matti's return to work, a load of slate broke from a hoist, and one of the slabs struck Matti in the legs, permanently crippling him. From then on, the family lived off Matti's small pension from the company.

Matti and Loviisa had always been nineteenth-century people, and now they discovered that they could not afford the twentieth century. If they needed to be somewhere, they walked or they drove the team of horses that Matti used for plowing in the winter and for farmwork in the summer. They got their water from a well. They retrieved the water with a handmade oaken bucket and a long rope. They had no electricity and used kerosene lanterns. They used an outhouse and bathed in a primitive sauna with a dirt floor. They scythed the grass in the yard and made their own foods—salting their own pork, smoking their own hams and fish, making their own yogurt and sweet cardamom bread, canning and jamming, and preserving fruits and vegetables in a root cellar. Their potato crop became a family mainstay.

Their children were all intelligent but not prone to emphasize academics. At home, the family spoke only Finnish, and practicalities came first. The boys hunted and fished winter and summer and ran trap lines. The girls berried and canned, cleaned and cooked. Everyone in the family knew farm work.

Matti and Loviisa's level-headed and hard-working children turned into tragic figures in adulthood. Maybe it was because Loviisa resembled an Eskimo, never learned English, and remained an outsider all her life. Certainly these were reasons that she drank. Maybe it was because Matti was a crippled ex-miner whose deafness caused him to shout his way through all conversations. Maybe it was just the combination of poverty and foreignness that haunted the children in adulthood. Whatever the reasons, they all had a hard time dealing with the world. The oldest girl, Lempi, died in her twenties of unknown causes far away in Boston where she had gone to work as a maid. The oldest son, Toivo, said that he could not live in a town without a bar and moved to Massachusetts. There he married, had children, and slowly drank himself to death. Aina had a son by an abusive miner, went insane in her late thirties, and spent the rest of her life in a state hospital. Lenni worked in the pits for a while and then volunteered during World War II. He fought in one battle after another from Normandy Beach to the Brenner Pass in Austria, and, when he returned to the farm after the war, he was a strange, withdrawn man. He never worked again. In fact, he never did much of anything. He stared into space for hours at a time. He drove all visitors except his younger brother Ahti off the family farm with Finnish oaths and a sharpened pitchfork. The youngest girl, Helen, married a good-hearted but often drunk miner who spoke a weird combination of Finnish and English and who often could not be understood in either language. And Ahti became a butcher.

Ahti dropped out of school in 1918 after completing the sixth grade. He began a meat-selling business, going door to door with a horse-drawn cart. Soon he graduated to a succession of pick-up trucks and widened his sales to the surrounding communities. The sides of native beef, chops of veal, legs of lamb, quartered hogs, chickens, and organ meat were kept on great blocks of ice that covered the truck bed. Beneath the ice blocks, a layer of sawdust absorbed the blood. The truck bed was enclosed, and whole bolognas and wheels of cheese sat on shelves or hung on nails along the walls. Most of the meat came from the family farm or other local farmers. Ahti slaughtered the animals himself, skinned them, and carved them into desirable roasts, steaks, and stew meats. He made complete use of the animals, saving the hides for tanning and using the heads and lips for cheese. He made sausage from the blood. He was a kind of artist with a butcher knife. He could slice the whole bolognas into individual slices with great rapidity, every slice of the same thickness.

In 1936, when he was thirty, Ahti married Anna. She was twenty and a teacher fresh out of Castine Normal School. She was from an old New England family and fulfilled Ahti's desire to be accepted as a one-hundred-percent American. Anna's family could trace its roots back to the Revolution and beyond. Her family was Unitarian but puritanical. No one in the family was allowed to work on Sunday, drink, smoke, or swear. The family patriarch, Orchard, had never allowed his daughters to do anything that he considered to be dangerous or unladylike. So Anna had never learned to swim or to ride a bicycle. She had also never dated.

Anna's family didn't just know a lot of history; they saw themselves as representatives of history—as the people that history was about. One of their ancestors had founded the town of Lee, Maine. They had little use for Finns who, from their perspective, had no history. The family also had little regard for other interlopers—for the tourists that invaded Maine every summer, for the French-Canadians who cut down the state's forests, for the other immigrants of non-British stock who had arrived in Maine with the Finns.

Ahti and Anna bought a house on a dead-end street on the east side of Monson. Behind the house was a small pasture, and beyond the pasture was a roadless forest that stretched all the way to Quebec. The uninhabited forest was divided into nameless township allotments that still carried the numbers given before 1820, when Maine was part of Massachusetts. Ahti would sometimes go fishing in Eighteen or maybe in Eleven, or he might spend a weekend hunting in Seventeen.

Anna's home became her realm. She was a wonderfully competent homemaker. At least once a week, she cleaned every nook and cranny of the house. She produced balanced meals three times a day. Every Saturday morning, she put a pot of beans to baking in the back of the wood stove's oven, and then she fried doughnuts and baked breads, cookies, and pie. She also prepared, painted, re-arranged, and repaired. She insisted on having the latest model refrigerator, a clothes washer and dryer, a freezer, and indoor plumbing. Ahti was happy to supply her with these signs of material wealth. Anna saw each new appliance as separating her from the Finns who lived in the other houses on the street. The Finnish women still washed clothes in tubs, still kept food cold in the cellar, and still did their personal business in an outhouse. "I will not live like a Finn," she told Ahti.

Soon Ahti and Anna had a daughter, Sirkka, born in 1938, and a son, Erkki, born in 1942. During World War II, the big meat-packing plants shipped their meats overseas to the Armed Forces, but Ahti had his own supply of meats, and his business boomed. Late in the war, the son of a local store owner was killed in France, and the owner became depressed. He no longer saw any purpose in spending his days behind a counter punching out numbers on a cash register. "I'll sell you the place cheap," he told Ahti.

In 1945, Ahti became the proprietor of a small grocery store. The store was popular with Finns because Ahti stocked their foods. He still slaughtered his own animals but now sold the meat in the store. He still made his own blood sausage, salt salmon, and pickled tripe. He spoke the customers' language and generally understood their wants. Most of his profits came from beer and other alcoholic products. On Sundays, he sold a dozen or more cases of vanilla extract (68.5 percent alcohol) because Sundays were dry statewide. After church in the summer, the miners gathered along the lakeshore behind the store and passed around the small extract bottles. They drank down the highly perfumed stuff as if they were tossing down shots of vodka. They threw the empty bottles into the lake. The water was shallow and the bottom muddy. Thousands of the tiny bottles lay scattered over the lake bottom. On sunny days, they glistened like stars.

Although the store was highly profitable, Ahti felt out of place there. He dreamed always of running away. "What I'd really like is a cabin in the woods," he told Anna. "One room and a dirt floor. That's good enough for me." He also dreamed of being a prize fighter. "When I was a boy, we used to make a rope ring out in the pasture and invite the neighbor boys over. I'd lick 'em all," he told his wife. He wanted to lick the whole world and then retreat into his cabin. Instead, he went to his store where he listened passively to the banter of the miners and to the pleadings for credit of the wives. He reached for his dream of freedom in the outdoors only rarely, when he hunted on Sundays in the fall. Hunting on the sabbath was illegal in Maine, but Ahti would not obey a law that infringed on his God-given rights. "God made bear and deer to be hunted long before He made Lutherans and Congregationalists and their laws," he argued when Anna objected.

Anna objected to a lot of her husband's world. She objected to the barn's contents. The barn, with its dozens of fat brown spiders, was full of Ahti's Finnish past. One corner where the floor was missing contained a combination sauna and smokehouse. The pile of sauna stones sat on a rusty iron grate that bridged a hollowed-out area in the dirt floor. The barn contained dozens of things that Ahti had brought from Matti and Loviisa's farm—harnesses for horse teams, saddles, tools for repairing buggy wheels, wrenches for Model T's, scythes, bucksaws, axes, anvils, tools for harrows and hay rakes, rakes with wooden tines, butcher knives, pulleys, weights, scales, bear traps, ice fishing flags, a rusting milk separater, a butter churn, butter molds, rifles, shotguns, shells, bows, arrows, leather aprons, horseshoes, a tool for bending and shaping the tips of skis, white Finnish Army skis from the Winter War, homemade snowshoes, homemade ski harnesses, a cider press, a moose sled, tanning vats, pickling barrels, molasses pumps, decomposing hides, cow and sheep skulls, kicksleds, ice tongs, cant hooks, and a wide variety of discarded men's hats. One quarter of the floor area was reserved for stove wood.

Anna also objected to visits at Matti and Loviisa's farm. "The place is dirty and dangerous, and I don't want my children there," she told Ahti, but, periodically, he drove his family there anyway. Anna always waited in the pickup with Sirkka and Erkki while Ahti went inside to talk to his parents in Finnish. The children were afraid of Matti because he always shouted in a foreign language. They were afraid of their Uncle Lenni because he appeared crazy, with a long, flowing beard and matted hair. The children were even afraid of their grandmother, who brought them homemade cookies and glasses of milk from her own cow. "Don't touch any of the food!" Anna ordered. "The cookies are surely full of germs. These people know nothing of hygiene," she told her children. Once, when little Erkki complained of thirst and reached for the milk, Anna slapped his hand hard. "You can have something to drink when we get home," she told him.

When Ahti's relatives or his Finnish friends visited Ahti, the wives waited in their pickups while the men approached the house. The men stood in the doorway or out in the yard and spoke quiet Finnish with Ahti. They did not come inside, for they knew they were unwanted there. That was Anna's realm.

In 1948, Matti had a lung removed. Except for a circle the size of a grapefruit, the removed lung was completely impacted with slate dust. Many of the miners expected a death from silicosis, and many were incapacitated by the time they were forty-five or fifty. Matti had not worked in the pits for many years, but the dust was still inside him. Matti lived a few more months before the other lung hemorrhaged, and he drowned in seconds. After that, Loviisa and Lenni lived alone at the farm. Lenni was not one to repair anything, and the farm buildings rapidly fell into disrepair. Ahti bought red paint and tried to get Lenni to paint the barn, but he opened all the cans and hurled each against the barn wall. The paint exploded against the wood, leaving great red circles as if the barn had an exotic form of measles. One night in midwinter of 1950, Loviisa came home late from drinking at her daughter's. A blizzard was raging, and Lenni had locked her out. She nearly froze to death. In the morning, Ahti drove to the farm on an errand and found his mother lying unconscious on the open porch by the front door. He rushed her to the hospital where one leg had to be amputated at the knee, and the toes and part of the foot had to be amputated from the remaining leg. For the rest of her life, Loviisa hobbled around on a crutch, looking to Sirkka and Erkki like a short and coppery version of Long John Silver.

From then on, Ahti paid the taxes on Loviisa's farm and paid his mother's hospital and living expenses. He also supported his brother Lenni, the son that Aina left behind when she was institutionalized, and occasionally Helen's family when her husband was jailed for being drunk and disorderly. Anna hated these extra expenses. "Your relatives will be the death of me," she told Ahti. She told her women friends, all of whom carried one hundred percent American names, that there had to be a lot of good Finns in Finland because "all the bad ones came to this country."

Once Sirkka and Erkki were in school all day and Anna was alone in her home, she felt more and more estranged from her neighbors. "I hate these Finns and Swedes for their petty jealousies and their ignorances," she told her few New England friends. Most of all, she hated them for their earthiness. She saw the first-generation Finns and Swedes as still trapped in the peasant mindset they had brought from Scandinavia. Anna admitted that they had some admirable traits —industriousness, parsimoniousness, and honesty—but she abhorred their weekend drunkenness, their lack of social graces, and their ignorance of the outside world.

Anna found Finnish incomprehensible and Finnish food disgusting. She prepared the same plain foods that her mother prepared. She refused to make any un-American foods except spaghetti and pizza, but her Italian cooking had a peculiar New England flavor. To prepare spaghetti and sauce, she boiled a package of elbow macaroni in a big pot, fried bits of salt pork in a frying pan, and heated a can of tomatoes. She drained the macaroni, dumped it back in the pot, added the tomatoes and salt pork, and served it. For pizza, she baked a pie crust and covered it with salt pork and another can of tomatoes.

Ahti abhorred the stuff and often prepared Finnish food, which he ate alone. Anna could not comprehend how anyone could eat fish roe in eggs, certain organs of an animal, or fish preserved in lye. Yet she had married someone who did. But still she recognized that she was blessed with an exceptional husband. He didn't drink, didn't dance the polka on Saturday night at the Finn Hall, and he didn't gamble. Mostly he worked. He opened the store every day, seven days a week at eight A.M. Usually he didn't close until eleven P.M. Although he was famous all over the countryside for the quality of his meats, he was rarely home.

When he did come home, Anna ranted at him, her mouth never closed and her voice never soft. She accused him of having no ambition, of never earning enough to satisfy her need to be socially above all of her neighbors. She blamed him for every little thing that went wrong. If the cellar flooded during the spring runoff, it was because he had chosen to live in such a God forsaken place. If a corner of the garden failed to produce, it was because he had failed to plant it properly. If he took an afternoon off in the summer to drive his family to a picnic area, he drove too fast or too slow or wasn't ready on time. In Anna's eyes, Ahti could never do anything right.

Anna used the fact that she had been a teacher before she married as the reason that she could not fit in with the miners' wives. She told him again and again that their worlds were small compared to hers. She read a lot—three or four thick books a month, mostly historical novels. She knew a lot of history, especially of Maine. She told her children about Benedict Arnold's march through Maine to attack Quebec. She told them about the fort on Penobscot Bay that was built during the War of 1812. "Those Finnish women are not interested in anything beyond their gardens, their canning, their housework, the town gossip, and Lutheran Church socials," Anna said to her friends at the Congregational church.

Anna's verbal attacks on her husband sometimes continued late into the night. Sirkka and Erkki often lay awake in bed and listened to her voice roaring like a storm through their small home. Erkki pictured his father nodding agreement or ducking aside, trying to make the barrage of words stop or go away. But it was all to no avail. She hated the town and blamed him for her unhappiness. Yet she, too, was to blame. She was paralyzed by her own sense of who she should be. She equated social success with marrying well. Marrying well meant, for a woman, never having to work. The miners' wives all did hard manual labor of one kind or another. They had to. Their husbands did not earn enough to support their families. The wives sold garden produce, berries, milk, and butter. They did other women's housecleaning or sewing. Many worked for the minimum wage in wood products mills. Anna saw herself as better than these women because she could stay home and be a housewife. At the same time, she hated the confinement of being a full-time wife and mother. She wanted more, wanted the stimulation of outside work. She threatened always to go back to teaching. Ahti acquiesced and said it would be fine with him if she went back to work. It would get her out of the house and bring in some more money and maybe get her off his back.

In 1954, the school district offered Anna a job and even offered to send her to the University of Maine so that her teacher certificate could be updated. For a week, Anna paced nervously about her kitchen and cuffed Sirkka or Erkki beside the head when they got too close to her. When Ahti came home from the store, she attacked him with more than the usual vehemence, shouting at him late into the night and still attacking him after they had gone to bed. Somehow, she managed to blame him for her own inability to accept the position, for her own fears and insecurities. She used a Maine term for cabin fever and cried out that she had "gone woods queer" after years of entrapment in the house.

Finally, she called the superintendent and refused the position. She told him that she would feel out of place at summer school at the university because of her age. The superintendent tried to dissuade her, but she was adamant. Later, Ahti bought her a new coat and gave her the money to re-do the kitchen. He tried to tell her that it was okay, that he still loved her whether she worked or not, that it was her decision and, therefore, okay with him. He told her that they didn't need the money—that he had a store and made more than any of the miners.

Then she attacked him again, saying that she knew all along that she hadn't wanted her to work. He said that wasn't true, that she could do whatever she liked.

But she did nothing. She stayed in her kitchen and complained. Her life was governed by her kitchen. Always she was there—at the counter making pies or doughnuts or cookies or at the stove preparing a meal or circling the table as the family ate.

She was now in terrible physical shape—lumpy and bumpy, with pale, soft flesh, bulbous eyes, and frizzy hair. Rarely did she leave the house and then only to pull vegetables out of the garden, to dig dandelions or mustard for greens, to berry in pastureland owned by Ahti.

She never learned to drive. She couldn't swim. She had no interest in sports or recreation. She could do very little that was practical beyond her housework, her kitchen, and simple home repairs.

In most ways, she was a good mother, however, and Sirkka and Erkki loved and respected her for that. She fed them well, clothed them well, doctored them when they were sick. She surrounded them with books and tried to instill in them the need to know about a larger world. She tried unsuccessfully to pass on her hatred of the town, and in Erkki she fed the need to escape.

By the mid-1950s, the slate-mining company had nearly died. Only one pit was being worked. Eighteen others lay scattered about the town. They resembled huge eye sockets staring blindly at the heavens. Beside the dead pits were blue-gray tailing heaps—lifeless moonscape of jumbled rock and shale. Scattered everywhere were rusting equipment and sagging buildings with broken windows. The town itself lost population and shrank. The Baptist and Lutheran churches closed for lack of congregations. Still, on occasion, some unlucky miner would die a sudden and violent death—crushed by a falling slab of slate or plummeting to his doom when a cable snapped.

At such times, people like Anna absorbed their grief without fanfare and quietly attended the Congregational Church, where the music was cold and indrawn and the sermons were careful. The seedier families—those with too many children for their income, decaying homes, and junked cars in the yard—saw visions, were born again, and attended the Pentecostal Church where they wailed out their pain in emotion-laden hymns and fire-and-damnation sermons. Many of the

Finnish miners would gather somewhere with a case of beer and a fifth of vodka and would toast their dead comrade. Ahti would just go to work as usual. After these deaths, Erkki would often awake in a sweat in the silence before dawn. Only half awake, he would have visions of being lost forever among countless trees. He would sense the forest as a malevolent force creeping upon their home, entering his bedroom, and reclaiming its pre-eminent position in the world.

In 1956, Loviisa died. Ahti inherited the farm, but crazy Lenni continued to live there. Lenni passed the long winters in the small space that was once the pantry. In there, he had a cot, a wood-burning stove, a kerosene lamp, a Finnish Bible, the *Kalevala*, and a five-string kantele that he had gotten from the Raisanen family after Jorma, the musician, died. Lenni read from the Bible every day, but each evening he chanted verses from the *Kalevala* while playing the kantele. Outside the pantry, the farmhouse had become a shambles, with no glass in the windows, collapsed plastering, molding furniture, and warped floors. Lenni used the former kitchen to store firewood and used the former living room as his toilet. The remainder of the farm buildings were now gone. The barn had collapsed in the winter of 1954, and the sheds had fallen down that spring. The porch still stood but leaned sharply away from the house.

Lenni still kept his sharpened pitchfork ready by the warped front door so he could drive away all visitors except Ahti and Erkki. They were useful since they brought him food and clothing. Lenni was a wild and disheveled figure. Within days of receiving new clothes, Lenni's raments were again black from dirt and woodsmoke. The clothes rarely fit properly since Ahti got them as hand-me-downs from miners who had known Lenni in the old days when he worked in the pits.

Erkki or his father visited the old farm daily, bringing Lenni food, tobacco, and other necessities. Lenni spoke to Ahti in Finnish but to Erkki in a resounding English that sometimes sounded biblical and sometimes sounded like a bad rendition of the *Kalevala*. Sometimes for their visits, Lenni wore the moldering remains of Loviisa's Lapp hat. Lenni's feet were much too big for what remained of Loviisa's reindeer boots, so he tied them together and hung them around his neck like oversized amulets. "Here I am, a Lutheran Lapp Finn Jew," he said to Erkki on several occasions. "I am scourged by life, driven out of society by visions of the holocaust. A great medal bird will set the world on fire! The world needs a savior, a hero of old. Now's the time we need to sorrow. Now's the time for lamentation. The world needs Väinämöinen and his magical kantele. The world needs a real hero who can capture the elk of Hiisi and the swan of Tuonela."

Erkki did not see himself as a capturer of elks and swans. He didn't even like to hunt. His favorite sport was basketball. He didn't see himself as a player of the kantele either. He preferred to listen to Fats Domino and the Big Bopper on the radio.

After these visits with Uncle Lenni, at night in the shelter of his bed, Erkki had a recurring nightmare. A long silver bird flew out of the shrouded darkness of the forest behind the family home, floated through Erkki's bedroom window, and rested with terrible force on the very top of Erkki's head. Sometimes he woke up screaming, his body soaked in sweat.

Anna and Ahti worried about Erkki after these episodes. Erkki heard them in their bedroom, talking about him. Anna worried that Erkki would end up as crazy as Lenni. "One day he'll run away from us," she insisted, but Ahti scoffed at the idea.

"He'll outgrow these fears. It's just the dark," Ahti said.

By the time Erkki entered high school, he realized that his Uncle Lenni's craziness was somehow linked to the atomic bomb, Bible prophecy, and a yearning for the lost world of ancient heroes. It was obvious that Lenni had read Revelations too many times. Erkki knew of Revelations because the children of Pentecostal neighbors often mentioned it. Anna told Erkki that Pentecostals were as crazy as Lenni. "Anyone who believes that sort of thing is infantile," she said. Anna detested anyone who spouted theories of fire and brimstone and the end of the world. "Religion should be as rational as anything else," she explained to Erkki. "If it's not rational, don't believe it." Anna was a pillar of the Congregational Church. She directed the choir, taught Sunday School, and often invited the minister for Sunday dinner. She had always read the Bible religiously and had read Bible stories to Erkki and Sirkka when they were preschoolers. Now that Erkki was a teenager, however, he could see no relationship between Bible stories and reality, and he could not comprehend the convergence of his mother's rationality and her irrational belief. "I don't believe any of this Bible stuff," he told his mother on a Sunday morning when he did not want to accompany her to church. "None of it makes any sense. It's unscientific."

Anna was furious. She stormed from the bathroom through the house to her bedroom and back again, shouting out her fury. "You're just like your father!" she roared as she passed Erkki in the kitchen. "He's never been in a respectable church in his life!" Because Erkki didn't know how to handle his mother's anger, he just stood there, smiling weakly. Anna rushed at him and yanked his hair so hard that Erkki lost his balance and crashed to the floor. Still, he refused to accompany her. She went to church alone.

When Anna returned, she was calm. She listened. Erkki told her that he could see no difference between the rantings of crazy Uncle Lenni and the rantings of the prophets. "People who talk to burning bushes, build boats to hold two of every kind of animal, and walk on water are crazier than Uncle," he said.

The rational side of Anna agreed with everything her son said, but the other half still wanted him to go to church. "It's good for you," she insisted. "It teaches you right from wrong."

"I already know right from wrong," Erkki replied. "Church is the most boring thing imaginable. I hate it."

Their argument ended there. Over dinner, the disagreement faded away and was replaced by the rich pleasure of eating good steak.

The next Sunday, Anna let her son sleep late. By the time Erkki rose, she had already left for church. When she returned, she brought a book with her. She handed it to Erkki as she came through the door. "If you promise to read this, I won't ask you to go to church with me anymore," Anna told him. The book was called *Twixt Twelve and Twenty*, and the author was Pat Boone. "The minister says that this book will counteract any crazy ideas you might get from that trashy rock and roll you listen to," she said. "It will help you to be a good Christian even without church." Erkki hated the sickeningly sweet music of Pat Boone. Plus he hated the way the guy dressed.

"He wears white bucks," he said.

Sirkka was now a senior in high school, and for two years she had been dating the son of a Finnish couple. Anti was only two years out of high school, but already he had his own pulp truck and worked as a woodcutter for a paper company. Anna was horrified at the prospect of her daughter marrying such a man. "The young man works hard, but he's not good enough for you," Anna told her daughter. "What can you talk about with someone who spends his days cutting down trees? You should go to college and meet a nice teacher or doctor or lawyer."

"But I love him," said Sirkka.

"You don't know what love is," said Anna. "Love is hard work and a lot of drudgery. And that's what you'll get if you marry a Finn."

In Erkki's freshman year at Monson Academy, Sirkka eloped with the woodcutter, and the newlyweds moved to Connecticut where the woodcutter started a tree-removal service in Hartford and where Anna could be kept at a distance. At the Academy, Erkki escaped the boredom of unimaginative teachers and easy classes through books and sports. Erkki's reading lacked direction but generally concerned tales of romantic travel in exotic places. He read every new *National Geographic* from cover to cover, and in between obtained old volumes from the town library under a stairwell at the back of the fire station. From the same library, he got the medieval travels of Marco Polo, the pre-war travels of Richard Halliburton, and the turn-of-the-century travels of Teddy Roosevelt. For the first time, Erkki began a serious study of the *Kalevala*. He read the entire poem in the two-volume edition of the Kirby translation. *Maybe this book will explain what it means to be a Finn*, he thought as he turned the pages. *Maybe I'll know who I am.*

Erkki participated in every sport the Academy offered its fifty students. He was a third-baseman on the baseball team, a runner on the cross-country team, a downhill racer and jumper on the ski team, and a forward on the basketball team.

Basketball was the lifeblood of the school and the town. Friday and Tuesday nights, virtually the whole population packed the gym for home games. The gym was the town's pride, with its lacquered hardwood floor, its glass backboards, and its spaciousness. Teams from the other towns in the league played on eccentric courts in buildings that should have been condemned a generation earlier. In Jackman, the gymnasium was long and narrow with a ceiling so low that only close-in shots with very flat arcs ever reached the basket. The rest were out of bounds as soon as they caromed off the ceiling. In North New Portland, a three-foot-by-four-foot heating duct sat directly under one basket. The waves of rising heat distorted shots and burned legs and bottoms. In Athens, the gymnasium also contained the fire department. The fire truck sat less than a yard from an end line. At midcourt was a wood-burning furnace that spewed wood dust and soot constantly. By the end of the game, lungs burned and uniforms, hair, and bare skin were black. In two other towns, the gyms were so small that a player could rebound under the opponent's basket, turn, and fire up a shot at the other basket without looking like a fool. Erkki loved the tiny gyms because scores were in the hundreds, and his individual average shot up.

The team's most absurd game was a sort of unoffical scrimmage arranged by the coach. The coach's friend had organized a team at an isolated hydroelectric dam eighty miles from anywhere by dirt road. The team journeyed to the dam in January, traveling through forests on permanent lease to paper companies. The private roads were periodically chained. At each chain, the coach had to explain their destination to a bored gatekeeper. The school by the dam had no gym—only an outdoor playground court with tin backboards. The snow had been bulldozed off the court and piled along the end lines. The wind was whistling loudly and the thermometer by the school door read five below zero. The team played in heavy clothes, including winter jackets, wool caps, and gloves. The coach told Erkki and the others not to run fast and not to jump. "If you fall on the ice, you'll break something," he warned them. "Don't throw the ball hard, dribble as little as possible, and try not to slide into anyone."

A month later, the team invited the guys from the dam to join one of their practices. The dam team was awed by the size of the gym but found it almost impossible to shoot well without wearing gloves.

Ahti occasionally closed the store to go and watch one of his son's games, but he understood little about basketball and afterwards found he had nothing to say to Erkki. Father and son were different in virtually every way. Ahti still went each fall into back fields and abandoned orchards to hunt deer. He still trapped bear and fished for trout in the stream at the head of the lake. He also liked to garden and to get in the winter's firewood. Erkki did these things too, but reluctantly. Erkki preferred American sports. He followed the Red Sox, the Packers, and the Celtics. Ahti knew nothing about these teams. Plus, Erkki was always reading. He was fascinated by American history and literature. Ahti read only the local paper and got the rest of his education from watching professional wrestling and boxing on TV.

Ahti wondered if he would ever be able to communicate with his son. *The trouble is that I'm a Finn who happens to live in America*, he thought. *Erkki is an American who happens to be a Finn.*

All through high school, Erkki dated a Finnish girl named Ingrid. Ingrid's parents were very proud of their heritage and instilled that pride in their daughter. Ingrid had spoken only Finnish before she went to kindergarten and could still speak a stilted and childish version of that language as a teenager. She was surprised that Erkki could speak no Finnish. "You don't even know how to say hello to your own relatives in their language, do you?" she asked him. Erkki admitted that this was true. "How can anyone who is so smart be so stupid?" she asked him. So Erkki sent for a Finnish grammar book and learned a few basic greetings. Ingrid was not impressed. "Being able to read *Tervetuloa* off someone's door mat does not make you a Finn," she told him.

Because Erkki was a ballplayer and Ingid was a cheerleader, by the strict code of high school, they were meant for each other. But they had little in common beyond sexual attraction. Ingid was not a reader, was not interested in one day going to college, and was not the sort to engage in stimulating conversation. Mostly she offered companionship and a good time while she checked out the men in her life to see which would make the best husband. She did not count Erkki as a good prospect. "You need to go to college because you don't know how to do anything," she told him.

Mostly, Erkki and Ingrid discovered the mystery of each other in the back of Erkki's 1950 Oldsmobile. In the dark recesses of lovers' lanes, Ingrid exuded a raw and earthy sexuality. Her blonde hair fell with the weight of rope below her waist. Her overlarge blue eyes stared roguishly out of a round smooth face dominated by overfull lips and high Mongolian cheeks. She liked to wear open peasant blouses that magnified the rich fullness of her breasts. She liked skirts that hugged the broad curve of her hips.

Ahti was delighted to see his son with a girl who could speak Finnish, but Anna warned Erkki to be careful. "If you get that girl in trouble, you'll be stuck forever inside this little town. You'll work yourself into an early death down in the mines, but even before that, your spirit will die as mine has died, and you'll become a kind of living dead."

"You sound as crazy as Lenni," Erkki told her, but he knew that she was right. In daylight, he and Ingrid stumbled around each other. Only in the darkness and the mystery of sex could they communicate.

Early on Saturday morning, a week before Erkki was to graduate with honors as a member of the class of 1961 of Monson Academy, Uncle Lenni appeared at Anna's back door. Ahti had already gone to work in the store, and Anna was terrified by Lenni's shoulder-length hair, scraggly beard, and filthy clothes. *Thank God*, she thought, as she noticed that he was not waving around his sharpened pitchfork. Instead, he held his kantele under his arm. "I want to speak to Erkki," Lenni told Anna. "If he's in bed, get him up. It's important."

Anna could not imagine Lenni ever saying anything of importance. She had a strong urge to call the neighbors and have Lenni thrown off her property, but she resisted the feeling and went to get her son.

While Anna watched warily from a distance, Lenni commanded Erkki to follow him into the barn, where they were immediately swallowed up by all the junk from Ahti's past. Lenni pointed at the bear and beaver traps rusting on nails along one wall. "Do you know how to use these?" he asked Erkki.

Erkki admitted that he didn't.

Lenni pointed to the sauna. "Do you know which stones are best for heating the sauna?" he asked.

Erkki said he didn't.

"Do you see how all of this stuff is your father? Do you see its Finnishness?" Lenni asked.

Erkki said he could see.

"But you can't *do*," said Lenni. "You're not a Finn in the way you live life or understand it. You have let your mother kill your own past. She has trampled on our heritage. That woman is a witch—a Louhi of North Farm!"

Erkki said nothing.

"Next week you are done with boyhood. You will be going into the world. But you don't even know who you are."

"I graduate next week. This coming fall, I'll go to college," said Erkki.

"That's only a place full of books," said Lenni. "It won't tell you who you are. It won't make your blood sing. It won't make you a Finn."

"But it will make me smart," said Erkki.

Lenni spit. "When I was young, I wanted to go to Suomi College in Hancock, Michigan. I wanted to study theology—to become a Lutheran minister. Instead, I stayed here and worked the pits. Then I went to war and killed a lot of people."

"I didn't know that," said Erkki.

"Afterwards, I decided to be crazy because it was safer than being sane. But my craziness nearly killed my mother. She lost a leg and part of a foot because of me."

Erkki didn't know what to say.

"You too will be in a war," said Lenni.

"I don't think so," answered Erkki.

"Oh, yes," insisted Lenni, and he placed his right hand firmly on Erkki's shoulder as if were knighting him. "All sane young men go to war. And you're so sane it makes me sick."

Erkki pointed out that the country was not currently at war and that he was not prone to wearing a uniform anyway, but Lenni hushed him. Then Lenni thrust the five-string kantele into Erkki's hands. "Take this," he said. "From now on you'll need it more than I. They'll be coming for me soon."

"Who's they?" Erkki asked.

"The so-called leading citizens of this town think I'm a danger to myself and to their children," replied Lenni. "They're going to lock me away in the State Hospital for the Insane. I'll soon be with my sister Aina. I haven't seen her for decades. I wonder how she is." Lenni looked thoughtful as Erkki took full possession of the kantele and placed it under his left arm.

"How do you know they're going to put you away?" Erkki asked.

"Your father told me," said Lenni. "Ahti has been resisting their moves for a long time. Now they've won."

"But you didn't do anything," said Erkki. "And we take care of you."

"It's not good enough," said Lenni. "Soon I'll be gone forever and you will replace me as a lost soul—as a wanderer in a crazy world. You won't know who you are. When you get lost enough, play the kantele and sing the old songs from the *Kalevala*. Maybe you'll be saved. At least then you'll be a Finn."

The lesson done, Lenni left the barn, crossed the road, entered a broad field, and walked toward the woods on the far side.

Erkki watched him until he was out of sight. Anna, who had been observing the conversation from afar, now approached her son and asked him where Lenni was going. "I don't know," said Erkki.

"He's such a pathetic and ugly man," said Anna. "What did he tell you?"

"Nothing," said Erkki.

That summer, Ingrid attended a cosmetology course in Portland. In the second week, she met a Coast Guardsman, married him a month later, and, by mid-August, had moved with him to Florida. Erkki never saw her again.

At the University of Maine, Erkki was a poor classroom student but a wonder in the library. Each day, hour after hour, he prowled the stacks, passing reverently down ill-lighted corridors of books to pick out choice volumes. He was re-created, remolded, reshaped by dozens of romantic literary heroes. He read Melville because he and his fictional heroes roamed the world's seas. He read Hemingway, Malraux, and Camus because they and their fictional heroes moved effortlessly through a multiplicity of cultures, fighting the good fight and loving good women. He read Salinger and Kerouac because they and their fictional heroes got lost in the vastness of America, escaping the madness of civilization through flight. All of these authors reminded Erkki of his Uncle Lenni. Lenni, too, had fled the madness of civilization, but Lenni's flight had been purely an internal one. Now he was locked away inside hospital corridors outside Bangor. Erkki felt the need to take flight too—to discover for himself the rich life of the nomad. He longed to roam the streets of exotic and ancient cities and to survey with his own eyes the geography of America, Asia, Africa, and Europe. *Maybe it's the Lapp blood of my grandmother that pushes me toward a nomadic existence*, Erkki thought.

At the back of the literary stacks, Erkki found a dusty and rarely used desk that was isolated from all other desks in the library. In the dorm, Erkki's roommate played Chubby Checker albums most of the day. He was majoring in pulp and paper production and thought that James Bond thrillers were the only literature worth reading. So Erkki fled to the isolated library desk to study, to read, and to begin the long process of learning to play the kantele. He found the library's slim collection of Finnish literature and read all of the authors in translation.

In his junior year, Erkki took several classes from a Finnish-American professor of economics history. The professor had grown up in the Finntown of Butte, Montana, but had graduated from Suomi College in Michigan. The professor always went out of his way to be friendly to students of Finnish background, and Erkki was delighted to meet another Finnish-American who was an authority figure. The professor soon became Erkki's adviser.

Just before Erkki graduated, the professor called him into his office for some final advice. "As soon as you leave here, the government will draft you and send you to Vietnam," the professor said.

"But it's a foolish war without purpose," Erkki replied. "Plus, I made a sort of pledge to someone not to go to war."

"Not going to war makes you just like your ancestor," the professor said. "He came to America to avoid serving in the czar's army."

Erkki was surprised by the certainty in the professor's voice. "I myself don't even know why my grandfather came to this country, so how do you know?" he asked the professor.

The professor explained that when he was growing up in Butte, he had asked his parents and his parents' friends why their ancestors had come to America, and all had said that their ancestors were fleeing service in the Russian Army. "While I was at Suomi College," the professor added, "I surveyed Finns from all over the Upper Peninsula, and every one said the same thing—that their ancestor had come to America to avoid the Russian Army. Then, at a national Finnish festival, I interviewed Finns from all over the country, and they too gave the same answer. So, apparently, it's true in one hundred percent of the cases.

"You mean we're a whole country of draft dodgers?" Erkki asked.

"That's right," said the professor. "Except for when we're fighting Russians instead of just avoiding their draft."

The professor advised that Erkki find a job the government would consider draft exempt, so Erkki joined the Peace Corps. "Plus it satisfies my Lappish urge for the nomadic life," he explained. The Peace Corps decided to send Erkki and his kantele to Nigeria after three months of training in East Lansing, Michigan. The training staff explained to Erkki and the other future volunteers that they were being sent to the one country that was the hope of Africa. "Nigeria is the only part of the old British Empire where the parliamentary system has taken hold," they said.

But on the weekend in 1966 when Erkki and the others arrived in Lagos, all the political leaders but one were assassinated, and, a few weeks later, their replacements were murdered. Then mobs ran through the streets and into schools, hospitals, government offices, and businesses, butchering thousands of people in the north of the country. The rule of law disappeared. The part of the country where Erkki taught English seceded and formed the Republic of Biafra. Then the Biafran children began to die of *kwashiorkor*. Within two years nearly all of them under ten died with swollen bellies, spindly legs, and pure white hair.

When the volunteers were expelled from the country. Erkki and his kantele found a new teaching position on a central Pacific island, but the timeless culture of the island had recently collided with the modern world, and the modern world had won. People who had once been happy to live in thatch-roofed homes and to fish were no longer happy and no longer fished. People who for ten thousand years had never heard of the eight-hour day now sat at desks shuffling paper. The desk jobs were without purpose and were actually part of an elaborate welfare system directed by faraway Washington. The mobs of young people without jobs felt uprooted and empty, so every day they got drunk and vented their anger on Erkki and his students by attacking them with rocks the size of grenades and clubs the size of baseball bats.

Soon Erkki and his kantele fled across Asia toward Europe. As Erkki's commercial flight flew through the night over Vietnam, he could see B-52s bombing, the orange mushroom clouds blossoming up from below.

Erkki and his kantele stopped on the north coast of Cyprus to try to recover from all the murder and mayhem he had witnessed, but Greek fanatics murdered the archbishop who governed the island and then began a systematic persecution of Turkish Cypriots. A few days later, when Erkki tried to go for an early morning swim on the beach in front of his hotel, thousands of Turkish marines in full battle gear were storming ashore out of landing craft. Erkki went for a swim anyway, but, when he was paddling around in the surf, he looked seaward and saw that a huge naval armada filled the horizon. Erkki wasn't sure whether he should continue to dog paddle in the surf or run like hell to the hotel to see if his kantele was safe. He looked at all the weapons around him, and he looked into the fanatical faces of the soldiers. Then he decided to stay in the surf. *If anyone asks, I'll just tell them I'm taking my morning constitutional,* he thought. By mid-morning, the beachhead was secured, and Erkki was led back to his room by scowling soldiers.

In his room, Erkki felt profoundly alone and without definition. He knew he was tied forever to a very small town in northern Maine, but he also knew he could never be at home there again. He was rootless. His mother had succeeded in alienating him from his Finnish relatives and Finnish heritage. At the same time, Erkki's latent Finnishness separated him from his mother's people and her New Englandness. Erkki needed a community of his own kind.

Erkki knew he had to return to the United States. At the airport in Istanbul, another American traveler asked Erkki where he had been, and Erkki gave the man the whole sordid tale of his misadventures. "Which exotic places are you traveling to now?" the man asked.

"Hancock, Michigan," Erkki said. "My kantele and I are heading there to learn about my heritage."

In Hancock, Erkki noticed that street signs were in Finnish and that restaurants served Finnish food. Erkki enrolled in Finnish Studies at Suomi College. Two years later, he transferred to the University of Minnesota to get his Bachelor's Degree and then transferred again to get his Ph.D. in Finnish-American Studies from the University of Wisconsin. Erkki became a professor of Finnish-American Studies. In lectures, he taught his students that every one of their ancestors had come to America to avoid service in the Russian Army. When the students parroted back the correct answer on a test, Erkki felt fulfilled. At last he was an accepted member of Finndom. Uncle Lenni, now dead and buried in northern Maine, no longer had to rave at him from the grave. Plus, he could play chopsticks on the kantele, and one day, he thought, he would learn to play something Finnish—maybe a polka or a hymn.

The Pictures of Ahti

A T THE AGE OF FIFTY-TWO, Erkki lived in the Finnish-American community of Hancock, Michigan, and taught at a Finnish Lutheran college. He still felt insubstantial when he thought of his disconnection to the past. *I'm an outsider,* he often thought, *a kind of ghost. I'll always be one.* Erkki felt a great void inside, an emptiness that his current job and family could only partially fill. Erkki was now married to a woman who was half Finnish and half French-Canadian, but his wife had severed all ties with her Finnish father and his family years before Erkki met her after her parents' divorce. Now Erkki worried that their daughters would grow up cut off from their Finnish heritage.

It was midsummer, and four-year-old Charlotte and two-year-old Lucy were playing dress-up in the living room. Erkki sat at the dining room table and stared at the large picture of Ahti above the bookcase. Erkki's sister, Sirkka, had sent the picture from Connecticut. Sirkka had rescued the picture of their father from a wall of their childhood home in Maine during her last visit there before the place was sold. It was the only picture of Ahti that Erkki owned.

In the picture, Erkki's father was a young man—decades younger than Erkki was then. Ahti was down on one knee, proudly displaying a bear he had shot. Erkki's mother-to-be, Anna, held the camera.

In the picture, I do not yet exist, Erkki thought. *My sister, Sirkka, does not exist. And, of course, my daughters, Charlotte and Lucy, will not exist for well beyond half a century.*

The picture's background brought Erkki faint memories. It was the barn at Grandfather Matti's farm—the barn that had fallen down over forty-years earlier. Before it fell, Uncle Lenni had thrown open cans of paint at it, decorating the weathered boards with huge red circles that ran toward the ground.

The picture pulled Erkki deep into the past, into the world that preceded his existence. That distant world was Finnish. Somewhere outside the closed, narrow box of the photo, Matti and

Loviisa conversed in their incomprehensible language. They spoke of the farm—of working with horses, of drying hay, of canning, of gardening, of milking, of berrying. They spoke of making yogurt and flat bread and of slaughtering their own animals and salting the meat. Ahti had known how to do all these things. Ahti had made his own sausage and had trapped bear and shot deer.

Did Erkki's Finnish-hating mother take the picture? Erkki had difficulty imagining her as a visitor at Matti and Loviisa's farm. Anna had been a member of the Daughters of the American Revolution. Her roots and the country's roots had been the same. Some unknown ancestor of hers had crossed the Atlantic long before the Revolutionary War and had founded the town of Lee, Maine, before Maine even existed as a state.

Anna's family had always known with absolute certainty that they were right in all things. Anna had known this. She had known, therefore, that Finnishness had to be wrong since it was not a part of old New England.

But Ahti had been a very attractive man. Anna the photographer would marry him. It would be her great opportunity. He was handsome, strong, thirty, terribly shy, and had his own business. She was done with school, had begun to teach, but she was no one's idea of a beauty. She had a soft and sallow body as lumpy and bumpy as an old potato. Her eyes were weak and bulbous, and her hair frizzed. She had a violent temper, prejudices galore, and a long list of phobias. Frightened of much of life, she would blame these fears on Ahti. He would become, until he died, the eternal scapegoat.

Why did he marry her? Erkki wondered. *Was it her cooking? Surely that had not been enough. He shouldn't have done it. In the picture he looked proud and happy. He had shot a bear.* Erkki wanted to warn Ahti. Erkki stared at the picture and implored Ahti not to do it—not to conceive children in the womb of old New England.

Years later, Erkki recalled, *when I was just beginning school, Ahti gave mother's people money to buy a farm, and they never repaid him. He brought them sides of beef and whole pigs and lambs. He packaged the meat for them—sliced the tenderloins into steaks, sawed the ribs for barbecues, but they never acknowledged his talents. They were inside a wall two hundred years old. Anna was inside, too, but Ahti and his Finnishness were not.*

Later, Erkki and Sirkka—locked out from Ahti's' world by Anna—had chosen to reject her world and her family. They had stood alone in a kind of wilderness—not Finnish and not old New England. What were they? They were nothing. They were Americans.

Later, Ahti had driven too fast. He had carried Anna over a woodpile. That had been the first accident. In the second, he had taken her into a telephone pole. She had shattered her leg and hip. Doctors had inserted metal plates and screws. The trauma had brought on diabetes. The diabetes had eaten her legs and taken away her sight. She had become a sort of vegetable—physically helpless but with her keen mind and her bitterness still intact.

Ahti had died of a stroke standing at the kitchen sink in the family home in Maine when Erkki was forty-two. But, in the picture, Ahti was still alive. All the little deaths still lay ahead. *Detour, Father!* Erkki wanted to shout.

After Ahti's death, Anna sat helplessly and hopelessly in a nursing home in old New England. In her blindness, she would never see the picture of Erkki's handsome young father-to-be as it hung above the dining room table in Erkki's home in northern Michigan. She would never know that the picture was surrounded by Finnishness. In every direction, the street signs were in Finnish. The names of surrounding towns were Finnish. She would never know that Erkki's daughters ate Finnish breads—*rieska* and *nisu*.

In fact, she would never know that Erkki had daughters. She would die in the nursing home in Maine before they were born. She would drown in her own liquids.

Erkki broke from his reverie and called to his daughters. He had to drive them to their maternal grandmother's home in Chassell, where they would play with cousins for a couple of hours.

As they drove past Michigan Tech, Charlotte asked Erkki if he was thinking about her grandfather's picture again. Erkki admitted that he was. "You've been looking at the picture a lot, Dad," Charlotte said. "Where is my grandfather anyway?"

Erkki told her that Ahti had died a long time before.

Charlotte wanted to know why she and Lucy had not said good-bye.

Erkki explained that neither of them had been born yet.

"But, who is he?" Charlotte asked, and Erkki realized that she still lived in an eternal present and that the passing of generations still meant nothing to her.

"A long time ago, I was a little boy," Erkki explained. "Just like you are a little girl now. The man in the picture was my daddy, just like I'm your daddy now."

"And where is he now?" she asked.

"Time passed. I got big. He grew old and died. Now he's gone."

Recognition came into Charlotte's voice, and, for the first time and forever, she understood the terrible meaning of death. "I wish that Lucy and I had given him a kiss and a hug and said good-bye," she said. Her voice was tiny, like all the rest of her, and Erkki was overwhelmed by her innocent sensitivity. "Did you say good-bye and give him a kiss and a hug, Dad?"

Erkki lied and said that he had because it was easier than trying to explain that Ahti had lived far away in Maine and that Erkki had been in Michigan, and Erkki certainly did not want to explain why in his pain he had missed the funeral altogether.

Then it occurred to Erkki that if Charlotte had not understood who Erkki's father was, then maybe she didn't understand who her maternal grandmother was either.

So, Erkki set out to explain, using the same argument— that her mom had once been a little girl and that her grandmother had once been a mom just like her own mom. Then Erkki explained that her aunts and uncles were also her mom's brothers and sisters, just like Lucy was her sister.

Charlotte understood. "Wow!" she said. "You know a lot, Dad. Do you know all of that because you teach?"

Erkki told her it was the other way around, and that age had a lot to do with it. "As we grow older, we learn more and more," Erkki said. "But we understand less and less until we realize one day that we don't know anything. Then we have a kind of empty wisdom."

Charlotte didn't follow that. Erkki wasn't sure that he did either.

For a number of minutes, Charlotte said nothing, but, as they reached the outskirts of Chassell, she suddenly asked where her name came from.

Erkki immediately regretted not having given her a traditional Finnish name that would have linked her to Ahti, Matti, Loviisa, and distant Finland. Instead, Erkki and his wife had opted for a literary name.

Erkki explained that "Charlotte" was a very old name and very pretty and so was her middle name "Emily." "Charlotte and Emily were girls who lived a long time ago in a country called England," Erkki explained. "They were sisters who grew up to write books. Your mom and dad once read their books. We liked them and gave you the sisters' names."

"I want to read those books," Charlotte said.

"Me, too," added Lucy, who up to then had remained silent but who never liked to be left out of anything—not even something that would not happen for at least ten or more years.

"Someday I'll read them to both of you," Erkki said.

And I will, Erkki promised himself. *And someday they will probably know more about the Brontës than they will ever know about Finnish writers through translations. My daughters are now and always will be American. As I am. The process is inevitable and maybe for the best. But I will teach them of their ancestors so that they will at least know some-thing, even if Finnishness is only a faint blur on their American souls. I need to do that.*

They arrived at the grandmother's.

Sarah the Missionary
❧ ❦

The Triumph of Christianity:
A Lutheran Pens a Pagan

I SPENT THE YEARS OF MY GIRLHOOD in a lonely, weathered fisherman's shanty on the shore of Lake Superior in Michigan's Upper Peninsula copper mining country. The shanty belonged to my Finnish grandparents. Both had grown up next to the great lake and neither had ever lived anywhere else. The nearby copper mines were vast, empty holes chiseled in the earth. Long before my birth, these mines had been abandoned. Only the shafts and tailing heaps remained, attesting to activity of by-gone years. The shafts resembled eyeless sockets.

My grandfather had spent his life fishing on Lake Superior. I could never decide whether he loved or hated the lake. He called the great expanse by its Indian name: Mother of Waters, "The old Mother of Waters is kicking up a bad storm today," he would say as he sat in the small kitchen of his shack and listened to creaking ceiling beams. When the house shook from a sudden, sharper gust, Grandfather would smile and puff on his pipe. "She's out to kill us," he would say as he cocked his ear to listen to the solid slap of waves on shore. "That old Mother of Waters hates all of us. She's been trying to kill me for years, but she hasn't succeeded. I'm still strong enough to take her fish."

Grandfather's favorite memories were of the days of early winter freeze. Often in December, steady, powerful winds would blow from Canada straight across the lake. These would build awesome waves to hurtle at our shore. When the waves struck the rocks behind our house, the noise seemed to split earth and sky.

When I was about four years old, Grandfather carried me out to watch the December lake as it reached its full fury during a freezing gale. Grandfather held tightly to my waist so I would not be blown away. We stood on shore as a wall of water sped toward us. As the frothing water struck our rocks, screeching wind swept the wave into the air and a solid sheet shot over our heads. At that instant, the sheet turned to glistening ice crystals and the world changed into a rainbow. A glint of sunlight cut through moiling clouds and burst into myriad colors against the sheet. "She's gonna drop that damned ice wave right on our heads!" Grandfather shouted, but the crystalline wall rushed up and over us, leaving us inexplicably dry. It smashed into the beach behind us. Shards of ice, like bits of exploding mortar shells, plowed into the sand or buzzed inland fifty feet or more.

As the gale subsided, Grandfather carried me inside and placed me by the woodburning stove. I was shivering from cold and fear. "A fine display of God's power!" Grandfather exclaimed, his forehead drenched with sweat.

ᐤ ᐠ

Grandmother was a pasty-faced woman whose eyes burned fiercely throughout long winters. As howling wind shook the house, she sat stiffly by the kitchen stove and read the Bible. She relaxed by tucking herself into a tight ball in her favorite rocker. Thick layers of shapeless shirts buried her upper body, while loose folds of oversized trousers hid her legs. Grandfather and I tip-toed about the adjoining room. If we accidentally made too much noise, she clapped her Bible shut and disappeared abruptly into her bedroom, slamming and locking the door.

Grandmother spent many days in her room, shuffling out in broken-backed shoes to sip a little broth or to eat a bowl of yogurt. She rarely spoke to us, and we feared her unbending wrath. "Ever since we've been married, she's spent one week out of four in her room," Grandfather confided. "Her excuse for that was over a long time ago, but she still locks herself in. She's never forgiven me for the birth of your father."

"What was he like?" I asked.

"A bit like her," Grandfather replied. "Stubborn as hell. I think he imagined himself as a Hebrew patriarch trapped with a flock of wolves. He used to talk to God when he was a child—used to sit right by the stove and carry on long conversations with the Heavenly Father. It bothered me, but your grandmother thought it was wonderful. She encouraged him. 'Tell the Lord what you've been doing today, dear,' she'd say, and he'd commence to ramble. Whenever I tried to discourage that sort of thing, your grandmother would rush in a fury into her room, and your father would follow. They'd stay there all day, praying for my soul. Sometimes your grandmother would glare as if she could already see me in hell.

She'd tell your father he'd been conceived in sin and could save himself only by devoting his life to saving others. I couldn't get close to the boy. He slept with his mother until he was school age. She hovered around all the time. I took him in the boat a few times, but he always got sick. He had a weak stomach and lungs. I loved him, but he wasn't mine, I guess.

"What do you mean?" I asked.

"Well, of course he was mine," continued Grandfather, "But he didn't have my blood in his veins. It was all hers—the blood of a fanatic. She ordained him before his birth. It was natural for him to ignore the rest of life and go into the ministry."

"And my mother?" I asked. "What about her?"

"Your mother?" Grandfather's voice sounded far away and sad. "She was a good woman, Sarah. She wasn't here long, but she had a good heart. Your father married her at the seminary and brought her home a few days before your birth. I was fishing when her time came. I didn't realize your father wouldn't get a doctor. When I returned, they had her in the ground. She was pretty, you know—too pretty and fragile. A few days later, your father left for mission work in the Pacific. He's been there ever since—on some island with the beautiful name of Helen. He's converted a lot of natives to his brand of Lutheranism. I can believe that. He'd run a strict church."

"Why doesn't Grandmother like me?" I blurted.

Startled, Grandfather hugged me against his big chest. "Somewhere underneath that stony exterior, she cares," he said. "She doesn't know how to show love. She's always getting it mixed up with her version of the Bible."

"She doesn't talk much," I said.

"I guess she's been running scared for a long time," Grandfather replied. "She doesn't know how to accept you."

"Why not?" I asked. "I never hurt her."

"You're a girl," Grandfather said. "Your grandmother can't accept any other woman in her son's life—not even if the woman is a child. Also, there's another reason. Do you know what 'out of wedlock' means?" I nodded that I thought I did. "Well, you were conceived that way—though your parents married before you were born. Your mother loved your father. There was nothing unholy about the way you began. If anything is unholy, it's this house and the way we live. I know it's hard on you, but I'll do my best."

Grandfather grew serious, his voice quavering. He hugged me pro-
tectively. "I can't offer much except love and advice," he said, and
then he went on to teach me a very simple lesson. Strive to love
life. Look to Christ as an example. He told me we're all crucified
in one way or another, but the discerning person concentrates on
the myriad crosses of the surrounding crowd. Be a true Christian
and ignore your own cross. Act to decrucify others. Be the lonely
one who would have saved Christ from his own stubborn death,
even at the cost of salvation in the eyes of God. Grandfather told
me to seek higher things than pain and agony as self-justification.
Then he clutched me. His body shook with little tremors, while a
feverish heat burned right through my clothes.

"Are you a true Christian?" I asked.

Grandfather thrust me away, held me at arm's length and
stared into my eyes. "No," he said. "Far from it. But I love life.
That's the first step toward salvation anyway."

"Then who is a true Christian?" I asked, mystified.

"Nobody," Grandfather replied. "Least of all the ones who
insist they are."

ᴼ᷎   ᴼ᷎

Summer and winter, Grandmother covered herself in a
shapeless mass of baggy pants and flannel shirts, but she smiled if
the sun lit up the beach. On warm summer days, she and I sometimes walked the shore and picnicked in a little sheltered cove
beyond a clump of cedars. During one picnic, when I was approaching adolescence, Grandmother hugged me affectionately. I
was surprised because she rarely showed me that she cared. "Soon
you'll be a woman," she said to me. "Someday I hope you meet a
man you can love—a man who will give you children you can love.
I loved your father very much, from the moment he was born.
Maybe I loved him too much. I never let him be himself. Now he's
gone away from me. Forever maybe. I pray for his forgiveness, but
I don't receive it."

Grandmother shuddered and hugged me harder. I could
feel her heart flapping wildly against my chest. Then her mood
changed abruptly as if often did, and she thrust me away from her.
"You're going to be pretty. You watch out for men. Don't let them
expel their blasphemy into you!"

I wanted to run away, to hide in the mute cedar forest. The lonely, wind-swept shore frightened me.

❧ ❧

One evening when I was seventeen and a senior in high school, my grandparents were having another of their many disagreements concerning something that was never mentioned. I had learned to be quiet at such times. After my grandmother locked herself in her room for the night, Grandfather began to talk. "Your grandmother married me because I was a warrior," he told me that evening. "I was a pagan hero in my youth. The wild blood of *Kalevala* ran through me." That night Grandfather told me of his youth. He told me how he had fallen deeply in love with Aina, the blonde daughter of a neighboring farmer. This was before he had met Grandmother. He had spent many evenings at Aina's home, courting her on the couch and forming marriage plans. In the meantime, Grandfather had obtained a small boat and had begun to fish commercially on Lake Superior. He sold his catch locally to neighbors and to stores in nearby Coppertown.

A year passed, and the love of my grandfather and Aina intensified. Each desired marriage, but Grandfather still could not support a wife on his income. He began negotiating with another fisherman for a larger boat, complete with equipment. If he obtained it, he planned to propose. Aina, not content to wait, worried incessantly about the consequences of passion. She urged Grandfather to announce a marriage date, but he refused. In desperation, Aina gave herself to Grandfather on his birthday. "It was wonderful," he told me. "She was a beautiful, sweet girl—the best present I ever had." Afterwards, Aina proclaimed that they had to marry soon because she might have a baby. Grandfather recommended waiting to see if a child had actually been conceived. The lovers quarreled until Aina cried. She accused Grandfather of not caring, and then she left. Grandfather felt terrible. The next day, he visited his fellow fishermen to tell of his plight. The other fishermen offered Grandfather the larger boat that he desired, though the cost was dear. It would take Grandfather a long time to pay off the debt. Nevertheless, the transaction was completed. The next day, a Sunday morning in spring, Grandfather hurried to Aina's home to give her the good news. He left his small shanty after breakfast. The sun glowed in clear sky, its warmth soaking his shirt. He walked rapidly, leg muscles straining tautly.

He reached Aina's farm in half an hour. In the yard, he noticed Aina's father by the woodshed. He was splitting firewood with fierce intensity. His face—stiff and frozen—smoldered with pain. He struck the logs with such exertion that he split the chopping block in several places. "I need to speak to Aina," Grandfather said. Aina's father didn't look up, but tears rushed from his eyes. Aina was dead. She had gone out in the rowboat after breakfast. The boat had tipped over. Aina, a good swimmer, had set out briskly for shore. The spring water, still frigid from winter cold, had numbed her arms and legs quickly. She had sunk about two hundred feet off shore. Her father had watched in horror as she disappeared beneath the waves. Helpless, he could not swim.

For a moment, Grandfather was struck immobile. Then he crept into the farmhouse to stand hopelessly beside the bed where they had laid out Aina's body. Her hair was still wet, her face starchy and damp. "I just went insane," Grandfather said. "Shouting wildly, I ran outside. I snatched the ax from Aina's father and tore off down the road. I ran about five miles, maybe more. Blinded by tears, I saw nothing until I came to the crossroads on the road back toward my place. The Lutheran Church stood at this juncture, and the service was just beginning. Most local people were inside. The church was an important place in those days, and I was well known as one who did not regularly attend. I rushed at the building with a wild cry, swinging the ax around and around in an arc. I slammed myself against the doors, and they flew open with a bang. The minister had been about to ask the congregation to bow their heads in prayer, to thank the Lord God for blessings. My abrupt, disheveled entry into His temple startled the minister into shocked silence. The congregation too was stunned as I dashed up the aisle and swung the ax fiercely at the wooden altar. The blow knocked the altar into the front pew. Women screamed and small children wailed. Menfolk clutched families and shoved them toward the safety of the open doors. In a moment, everyone was scattering out of my way. I paid no heed because I was intent on punishing God. I jumped onto a chair near the back wall and swung at the wooden backdrop cross. I sliced cleanly through and it clattered to the floor. Turning toward the remaining churchgoers still pushing each other out the door, I began to shout, 'That son of a bitch gets no thanks from me. He deserves to burn in hell.'"

For a few minutes, Grandfather stood silently inside the abandoned church, consumed by impotent rage. Then he began to hack furiously at the altar. A few chips flew, but its solidity resisted his blows. Grandfather kicked over several pews and dashed at the stained glass windows. The windows brought him to his senses. They were beautiful—too beautiful to destroy. People had made them—not God. He began to sob harder and ran out of the church. On the lawn, the congregation scurried aside as Grandfather ran past them and down the road toward home. Along the way, he cast the ax into the ditch.

By the time Grandfather arrived at his shanty, he had cried himself out. He knew already that life would go on in spite of death and damnation. As soon as he walked through his front door, he felt exhausted. He staggered to his bedroom and collapsed into a deep sleep. He must have slept for several hours, for when he awoke it was mid-afternoon. He came out of the bedroom and put a pot of coffee on the stove. Just then the door opened and my grandmother came in. Grandmother was a young woman well known for her piety. She rarely missed a service and always carried a Bible somewhere on her person. She was visibly upset because she had seen Grandfather chop at the altar. Her face was ashen.

"Are you okay?" she asked.

"I'll live," he replied. "Aina is dead."

"I know," she said. "Aina is dead, and you have tried to kill God. That was a terrible blasphemy you committed."

"God committed a far worse blasphemy," Grandfather replied. "He deserves to be dead while Aina deserves to live."

"I want you to get down on your knees and pray with me," Grandmother said. "We must try to save your soul."

"My soul will take care of itself," he said, anger surging inside him. "Take your empty religion and go away!" he cried. "I don't need you."

"Need me," Grandmother pleaded softly. "I want you to need me." She advanced and put her arms around his waist. She began to kiss him all over—his face, neck, and chest. "I want to save you," she whispered. "I need to save you from yourself."

Before Grandfather knew what had happened, he had Grandmother in the bedroom and was making love to her. It was a strange, angry kind of love that contained all the pain and sorrow of his loss. Grandfather found himself caught up in an uncontrollable

desire to hurt her. "She cried out in surprise and pain, and I react-
ed by biting her neck," he told me in sad, hushed tones. "I snarled.
I desecrated the godliness of her young body. At the end, she
clawed my face. As I rolled away, she tore my hair in rage. She tried
to rip me apart, but I was strong. I kicked her from the bed, and she
struck her head on a corner of the closet. She lay on the floor,
stunned and whimpering. I threw her dress at her, and it struck her
face. She rolled her body into a tight ball and hid her face in the
crumpled cloth. I got dressed and fled. I ran for some distance
along the beach and then sprawled on a dune with my hands over
my head. I lay there for a long time. When I finally returned, your
grandmother had left. I didn't try to find her. Probably I should
have, but I was scared. By then my anger had subsided, and I had
had time to think. I knew the damage I had done to your grandmother and myself. She had only wanted to replace the woman I
loved, and, in doing that, she had made herself vulnerable. I had
taken advantage of that vulnerability. Plus, I had attacked God.
God had made the lake that drowned Aina, but Aina herself probably caused the boat to tip. God hadn't done anything. He had created. That's all. How could I blame Him for that?"

In July, Grandmother visited Grandfather again. She was
pregnant and wanted to know what he was going to do. He told her
he would marry her since he was an honorable man. She said she
would never forget how the baby had been conceived. "You raped
me," she said. "You were still killing God. You hurt me because I
am a God-fearing woman, and now I can't lie with you ever again.
If we marry, you must promise two things. First, we must have separate bedrooms. Second, our child must be dedicated to the service
of God without interference from you."

"That was a hard bargain," Grandfather told me, "but I
have stuck to it for over thirty years while your grandmother has
played on my guilt and shame. Still, life is good. The sun warms
the flesh, and the lake is an overwhelmingly beautiful but indiffer-
ent force—a kind of God without reason. The waters are most
beautiful when they are full of wrath. Remember, my daughter,
that life is lovely."

ב   ב

In high school, I pursued the business course, not because
I was interested in becoming a secretary but because the course left

me time to read. After graduation, I became a secretary in the Peninsula National Bank in Coppertown. The day I left, Grandfather helped me pack my few belongings. He drove me in his rusty pickup through the forest. I found an efficiency apartment a block from the bank and across the street from a college. A week later, I signed up for some night courses. My life settled quickly into a routine, but inside I was restless. The other girls at the bank were from Coppertown and viewed me suspiciously. I hated lonely evenings in my apartment on Portage Street. I could see no purpose to my job. A night course in literature interested me, but it wasn't enough.

At the end of my first month, another secretary introduced me to Matti. Matti had the light skin, blond hair, and athletic build of a Finn. His perpetual smile and fine features intrigued me. One noon the secretaries went to a nearby luncheonette during break. We were eating sandwiches and gossiping about work when Matti joined us. I asked Matti about his work, and he smiled wryly.

"Oh, I don't do anything," Matti answered. "Of course, that's not completely true. I do play basketball."

"What kind of basketball?" I asked.

"Oh, any kind," laughed Matti. "Really, that's the only thing I like to do. It doesn't pay, though, so I write."

"Novels?" I asked.

"No, nothing like that," Matti replied. "I write local stuff. Newspaper articles about the Copper Country. Right now I'm writing a long article about Isle Royale for a historical society." Isle Royal is a big island in the middle of Lake Superior and popular with tourists. A ferry runs there in the summer so people can use the hiking trails and see the wildlife—bear, moose, and wolves.

Matti invited me to his house on Saturday. He would pick me up at my apartment for a dinner date of smoked fish. I wanted to prepare a dish, but Matti insisted that he would prepare the whole meal. Curious, I asked what other foods he planned to have. "Nothing," he told me. "My friends will be there, and we'll just eat smoked fish and drink lots of beer."

"But what if I don't like smoked fish?" I asked him.

"All of my friends do," Matti replied. "Everyone eats smoked fish and drinks beer."

When I asked Matti what I should wear, he laughed. "All my friends wear tattered jeans," he said. "If you've got some, wear 'em."

Early Saturday evening, Matti drove me to his house, at the end of a rarely used county road. We drove miles along the dirt track, billowing brown dust obliterating our passage. We passed a lonesome radio tower whose tiny beacon glowed red above green forests. Soon we pulled to the side and stopped. Matti's home was a high, barn-like building—weathered and unpainted. I got out of the car with trepidation. In single file, Matti and I followed a narrow path around piles of rotting rubbish. Numerous small bushes and burdocks reached to the front door. In the middle of the yard, half-buried in high grass, a discarded refrigerator leaned at an odd angle.

Matti and I entered his house. The rooms were cavernous—high old-fashioned ceilings and oversized windows. A potbelly woodstove rusted beside a pile of neatly stacked wood. The building—once a country schoolhouse—had deteriorated for forty years. Several years before, Matti had received an inheritance from an uncle and had bought the building and its lot. He and his friends frequently held beer parties in the front yard.

Matti motioned me to follow. We passed through the house and jumped to the ground from a stepless rear door. A second path twisted toward a stand of cedars several hundred feet away. We walked through layers of yellow-gray hay into the stand. Soon we came to a lopsided, two-hole outhouse—the original facility. Matti swung the door open to reveal the graffiti of former school children. I began to laugh. "I once read about a man who had a door like that," I said. "He carried it from house to house, asking people if their names were there. He wanted to know the history of his door, of all the lives that had passed through it."

Matti thought that was extremely funny. "Some night when I'm drunk," he explained, "I might try that, though these names go back to the class of 1910 or thereabouts, and most must be dead by now."

When Matti and I returned, guests were scattered in the front yard among thornbushes, rubbish, rocks, and matted grass. Most were restless young men in jeans and flannel shirts with quarts of beer in their hands. A few were girls from the bank, secretaries like me. The crowd gathered in a circle around large boulders where someone had started a fire. Flames were burning briskly. A young man—too drunk to control himself—staggered away to retch loudly behind a small bush. Matti urged me to join the others, but I was cold. The sun was setting, and, in northern Michigan, the evenings were twenty degrees cooler than the days. I asked if I might borrow a jacket. Matti told me to look inside as he joined the crowd. I entered the house alone.

In the living room, an old fisherman sat in the only comfortable chair. As I searched unsuccessfully for a jacket, the fisherman introduced himself. He knew my grandfather, for they had fished together many times. He asked me why I was there, so I explained. The fisherman chuckled. He and Matti had gone fishing together earlier. Afterwards, he had given Matti a mess of fish. "But you won't eat any, my dear. Matti used that old refrigerator outside as a makeshift smokehouse, but he's too lazy to clean it. This afternoon, layers of old fish oil caught fire and burned everything."

The old fisherman leaned close to whisper. "The girls all work in the bank because there's nothing else to do. None of 'em like it. Mostly they're looking for husbands. These young men live off the girls, off their hopes and desires. Matti's like that. First he's with one, and then another. Some of the young men are mean, and all of them drink too much. A few can't find any women to support them, so they live off welfare. I tell Matti to get a job, but he just laughs. He's a nice guy, but never serious. He's lazy, with a wasted, pointless life. Don't get me wrong. I like Matti. He just drinks too much. He's been drinking all day, and look what he did to the fish. Burned them to a crisp. I hope you aren't a girlfriend, because he's not the marrying kind. He does only what pleases Matti. Keep that in mind."

The old fisherman rose to leave, so I joined the others. Stars came out and the ground grew damp. Everyone else was wearing a jacket and sipping beer. Open quart bottles lay scattered about, while a fresh supply sat in a huge heap beyond the fire. Shivering, I moved closer to the flames where a group was roasting hotdogs on sticks. Hungry, I took a hotdog from a package sitting on a rock. Someone handed me a stick. Self-conscious, I roasted the hotdog and ate it without bread. No one introduced himself. Several young men were drunk.

From beyond the fire glow, a middle-aged woman in a turtle-neck sweater approached. She thrust her busy hair close to my face and stared, without speaking, for several seconds. "Are you an educator?" she finally asked.

"No," I said. "I just graduated from high school. I work in the bank."

"Strange," replied the woman. "I thought I knew all the girls at the bank." Her voice sounded vaguely threatening, as if she were interrogating me about a terrible crime.

"I'm new at the bank," I replied defensively. "I've been there only a month."

"You look like an educator," the woman said. "Like an elementary teacher. I don't like them. They program people to fit the needs of this sick society."

"And who are you?" I asked.

"Me? I'm a bartender. An honorable profession. I'm also an unrecognized artist. Maybe an educator of sorts too. I believe everyone should do whatever he wants to do whenever he wants to do it. If I had a school, that's how I'd run it."

"Bravo!" cried a voice behind me. A long-haired, pot-bellied young man stood there, dangling a cigarette from indulgent fingers and cradling a bottle. "I went into teaching for a week. It's all bullshit. I quit and came home."

"Hi. I'm Sarah," I said. "What do you do now?"

The young man didn't introduce himself. He took a long drag on his cigarette. "I play ball with a bunch of guys from Harry's bar," he said. "We drink a lot."

"But what do you do to earn money?" I asked.

"I get the welfare," he said. "My girlfriend works at the bank. She's Mary. She says she works with you sometimes. She's thinking of quitting and going to Detroit. I don't know what I'll do then. Just live at Harry's, I guess.'

The man began a fervid conversation with the woman in the turtleneck. For a short time, I stood nearby and listened, but soon I realized that neither was any longer aware of my presence. Alone, I wandered in a slow circle around the bonfire, but no friendly faces approached. Matti ignored me. He now slouched on a log beyond the flickering fire. He was drinking whiskey. Feeling trapped in the slurred, drunken talk, I approached Matti and told him I had a migraine headache. He agreed to drive me home.

In the car, I realized Matti was too drunk to drive. After fumbling with the key, he managed to start the car. Then he put it into reverse instead of forward and nearly drove over the embankment. Frightened, I asked if he would let me drive, but he only laughed. "I'll get us there," he said and careened down the road.

As we approached the intersection where the narrow dirt road met the main route, Matti peered blearily over the wheel as if the windshield were glazed by dense fog. He entered the intersection, drove straight across it without braking and slammed into a cluster of trees. One tree sheared off a fender, while another twisted the frame grotesquely. For a terrifying moment, we hung over a low ditch. Then the car leaped forward and flipped onto its side. With a screech of torn metal, the car slid through bushes. Miraculously, we came to a stop. Immediately, I heard a series of soft popping noises in the rear. Flames lit up the darkness. The car's interior flickered from yellow to black as tongues of oily fire blinked off and on.

Matti pressed me against the bottom of the car. I struggled against his dead weight. As flames blinked to life again, I could see his face staring with mystification at the slowly spinning front wheel. "So this is how we die,"he said groggily. "It doesn't even hurt."

"I don't want to die!" I cried. "I don't want to die!"

Flames loomed brightly out of the engine. In horror, I perceived a strange face dancing in the flames. The hideous face grew to enormous proportions before it raced past my face, to disappear into the blackness. "I just saw my father!" I screeched at Matti. "In the flames! I want to go to the island!"

The word shocked Matti out of his drunken stupor. "The island?" he asked. "What are you talking about? Where are we?" Comprehension formed on his face, and his muscles tightened into action. He threw himself upward, his shoulder catching the crumpled door with a jarring blow. The door swung open against its own weight, and stars shown brightly from above. As I pushed from below, Matti stumbled up through the opening, lost his balance, and rolled across and off the upturned side. His body thumped against the ground. A moment later, I crawled up through the twisted doorway. In the darkness, I stumbled. Crying, I dropped into the bushes. I sprawled on wet, soggy ground beside Matti—still stretched as he had landed. His body, loose and inert, could not be moved. "Those flames may catch the tank and explode!" I cried. "We've got to move further back!" I yanked at his shoulder, but he pulled away in irritation.

"Damnit!" Matti shouted and staggered to his feet. "How in hell did that tree get in the road? Why is there a son-of-a-bitching tree right in the middle of the road?" He lost his balance again and fell forward, sticking his face into the growing flames. Blistered by the heat, he crawled away through the trees. I staggered after him. Behind us, flames leaped like phantoms. I located a large birch, and Matti propped himself against it. I asked him if he were hurt. He said nothing. Although bruised from my fall and bleeding from small cuts, I was in pretty good shape.

As soon as I was safe, my fear turned to anger. I boiled with fierce hatred for Matti, who had almost killed me. "Damn you!" I shouted in his face. "All I want is to get out of here! Out of this damned area! It's pointless! I've never seen my father! I want to go to the island—his island! I don't want him to just be a myth somewhere far away! I must escape to the island."

"Island," muttered Matti, and the word hung on his lip, refusing to go away. "Island," he said again. "I never heard of such a thing. What I want to know is . . . how in hell did we get to Isle Royale? You ought to know. You're not drunk."

"What gibberish are you spouting now?" I asked.

"The island. You said something about an island," Matti said and passed out.

I huddled under the birch with Matti's inert form for twenty minutes. Then a police car pulled up. The two officers came down the embankment, their flashlights beaming. I shouted until the sharp beams swung in our direction. Blinded by the glare, I thrust my hands over my eyes. Revived by the light, Matti began to shout. "Turn off the damned light! I can't sleep with that damned light in my eyes!" Then Matti realized that two policemen stood behind the lights. Using the birch for support, he slowly pushed himself upright. "Good evening, gentlemen," he said good naturedly. "Don't go away because I have a very important question for you . . . and the question is this . . . how in hell did this young lady and I get to Isle Royale? How did we cross Lake Superior in my car?"

"What are you talking about?" said a policeman.

"Suddenly there it was—this damned tree right in the middle of the road, and I says to myself, 'That explains it, Matti. Only on Isle Royale would they have a damned tree right in the middle of the road.'"

"He's either stark raving mad or dead drunk," said an officer.

"He's drunk all right," said the other policeman. "I can smell him from here. What about the girl?"

"I'm not drunk," I said. "I never drink. I just want to get out of here. I want to go to my father's island in the Pacific Ocean."

"She sounds loony," said the first policeman.

"You don't understand," I said. "I just want to get out of here."

"You should," said the second officer. "You and your drunken friend have been sitting in a puddle. This is swampy ground all over." His light scanned my clothes, soaked in muddy water and covered with bits of grass and moss.

We moved as a group to the police car. Matti slept while the policemen drove him to jail. Then they took me to my apartment.

I never saw Matti again. The next day, I quit my job and got a ride back to my grandparents' shanty on the lake. Grandfather had put aside money for my education, so I asked if I could have it. He was surprised when I told him I wanted to be a missionary. "Don't worry," I told him. "I won't be like my grandmother and father. I just want to get to my father's island. I've never seen him. How else could I get there? Anyway, you told me yourself when I was a little girl that Jesus was the most remarkable man who ever lived. I agree. I want to teach people about his life. I agree with you about something else, too. God's creation is lovely. Especially the lake."

Grandfather smiled. He approved. "Only a loving God could make something so beautiful," he said, surprising me. "Don't look so shocked," he added. "Remember, my quarrel with the Creator was over a long time ago. The lake giveth and the lake taketh away. Unfortunately, your grandmother has never forgiven me for my youthful folly in her church so long ago, and she'll never forgive me for what happened in the bedroom afterwards."

∂ ∾

Grandfather hugged me the day I left. Grandmother said that she couldn't bear to lose another child. She said she was being driven mad by loneliness. She locked herself in her room. Before I left, I said good-bye through the closed door. That was sad because I wouldn't see her for a long time. But I would come back. And I would try to bring my father with me.